CW01506708

She Was Never Your Wife

Staccato-Paced
Psychological Thriller

D / T / N

CHAPTER 1

QUIET VACANCY

Lucas surfaced from a dream that left no aftertaste.
Blank mind.
Bare senses.
He stared at the ceiling, letting the soft grey of pre-dawn arrange itself into shape.

Then he rolled to his right.

Nothing.

An untouched pillow.
A quilt still folded along its manufacturing crease.
The faint scent of lavender fabric softener, but no warmth, no exhale, no absentminded hum.
He pressed his palm flat against the sheet.
Cold cotton met his skin—a temperature reserved for objects, not bodies.

A sting of alarm grazed him.
He sat upright.
No indentation.
No stray hair curled against the white case.

On the bedside table, her wedding ring waited—thin gold band, almost weightless, usually a permanent gleam on her left hand.
Now it lay as if placed with surgical care, exactly

centered on the coaster that held her nighttime water glass.
The glass itself was gone.

Lucas slipped from the mattress, bare feet meeting hardwood that had cooled overnight.
The bedroom held its usual order: his leather wallet on the dresser; a pair of slacks folded over the valet chair; Julia's side table stacked with half-read novels.
Yet the room felt dislocated, like a set before actors walk on.

"Julia?"
He spoke her name into the hush.
The syllables landed without echo.

He crossed to the ensuite.
The door hung ajar in habitual invitation.
Mirror dark; only a single moon-white bar of motion sensor light above the sink.
Two toothbrushes stood inside a ceramic beaker—his electric blue, her soft-bristle coral—side by side like silent sentries.
But her travel cosmetic pouch, usually zipped and perched behind the faucets, was missing.
The dampness from her nightly face wash had already dried.

Lucas paused, letting a thin pulse of dread fan out under his ribs.

Kitchen next.
He flicked the light.
The bulb stuttered, then glowed.

Countertops empty except for the French press she favored; no grounds, no steam.

The red ceramic mug with its chipped lip—her mug—was absent from the rack.

The fridge door seal let a sigh when opened.

Milk, eggs, a Tupperware of leftover lentil soup, everything in place.

He opened the drawer where they dumped keys, receipts, random euro coins.

His house key sat alone like a single tooth.

Hers was gone.

So was the fob for the building's underground garage.

Lucas's heart thudded in the parallel rhythm of panic and disbelief.

He padded to the living room, switching on lamps as he went, trying to paint the night away with domestic light.

Couch cushions undisturbed.

Blanket folded.

The remote precisely aligned with the coffee-table edge—the way he left it before bed.

Julia's reading glasses, however, were missing from their habitual roost atop the bookshelf.

He grabbed his phone from the wireless charger beside the sofa.

Black screen.

He pressed power.

No response.

Battery had been ninety-two percent when he lay down at midnight.

Now it behaved like a dead stone.

He carried the inert device back to the bedroom,
plugged a cable straight into the wall socket.
Still nothing.
No charging icon.
No flicker.
A deliberate sabotage?
The thought arrived too quickly for comfort.

He pulled on sweatpants, feet forced into trainers
without socks, and returned to the foyer.
Pressed an ear against the apartment door, listening
for hallway noises: the elderly couple upstairs starting
their radio, the paperboy dropping copies by each flat,
the elevator's hydraulic yawn.
Only silence.

Lucas unlocked, cracked the door, peered down the
corridor.
Carpet pristine.
No wet footprints, no stray envelope.
The corridor light hummed, indifferent.

He shut the door, bolted it, feeling absurd for securing a
space already looted of its most precious occupant.

Panic edged toward anger.
He picked up the landline—an anachronism kept
mostly for Julia's fondness for rotary nostalgia—and
dialed her mobile.
Three electronic beeps, then a recorded voice in Czech
announced the subscriber was unavailable.
No voicemail greeting, because Julia hated recordings
of herself.

He dialed 110.

An operator answered in measured German.

Lucas gave name, address, explained his wife was missing.

The operator asked how long she had been gone.

He checked the bedside clock: 06:14.

Julia had kissed him goodnight at 00:07; he remembered because he'd teased her about the palindromic time.

"Roughly six hours," he said.

The operator exhaled softly, audible through the line.

"Sir, the official threshold for a missing-person report is twenty-four hours, unless there's evidence of foul play or immediate danger."

Lucas's grip tightened on the receiver.

"I woke up. She's vanished. Her ring is here. Her phone unreachable. That feels dangerous."

"I understand. Perhaps she stepped out early?"

"She took all her clothes but left her toothbrush," he said.

His words sounded insane even to him.

"Is there a history of tension in the relationship?"

The question rattled him.

"No," he replied, then softer: "Not enough to erase a person."

The operator suggested he visit the station to file a preliminary note, just in case.

She promised to log the call time.

They disconnected.

Lucas replaced the handset with unwilled gentleness, as though noise might shatter the spinning glass of his thoughts.

He returned to the bedroom, flung open Julia's wardrobe.
Gaping emptiness.
Hangers clacked when jostled, a brittle castanet.
Every dress, cardigan, pair of jeans—gone.
But on the shelf above, her folded funeral dress remained: black crepe, still sealed in its dry-cleaning plastic.
He touched the plastic; it crinkled like a joke told too late.

He crouched, scanning the floor of the closet.
Her ballet flats absent; hiking boots missing; suitcases no longer stacked in nesting order.
In their place, vacuum-shaped rectangles of dust where the suitcases had protected the wood.

Lucas stood, head throbbing from adrenaline spikes.
He yanked open the linen drawer beside the bed, searching for some scribbled note, some anchor of explanation.
Nothing but spare pillowcases, lavender-scented sachets.

He swallowed, noticing for the first time the swell of morning light creeping under the blinds.
Dawn insisted on proceeding.
Oblivious.

He paced the apartment, trailing his right hand along the walls like a man mapping memory with fingertips. No stray earrings, no perfume bottle, no scarf on a chair back.

Julia had been extracted with surgical thoroughness, save for curated relics: the ring, the toothbrush, the funeral dress.

And, he realized, whatever might lurk beneath surfaces he rarely disturbed.

He knelt beside the bed again, lifted the hanging valance, and peered into the under-bed gloom.

Cardboard boxes of tax files.

A shoebox of old Polaroids.

Dust bunnies.

And something flat, plastic, reflective.

Lucas reached.

His fingers closed around a bank card.

EU blue.

He squinted at the name embossed in silver.

KAROLINA VONDRÁKOVÁ

Not Julia Schwarz.

Not a variation.

Entirely foreign.

He turned the card over.

Česká spořitelna—Czech Savings Bank.

Expiration next year.

A tiny chip, unscratched.

He pressed a thumb against its glossy face, half expecting it to dissolve.

Lucas sank back on his heels, card balanced on his palm like a fragile insect.

Who was Karolina?
Why was her EC card beneath their marital bed?
Had Julia hidden it?
Dropped it while packing a stealthy exit?
Or had someone else crawled under here and left it intentionally, like a breadcrumb pointing further into the forest?

He stood too fast; dizziness smeared the room.
The card felt oddly warm now, or maybe his hand had gone cold.

He straightened, pocketed the find, and crossed to the desk where Julia kept a small fireproof safe.
Combination lock.
He spun the dial: her late grandfather's birthday.
Safe opened with a sigh.

Inside he expected passports, insurance papers, maybe the odd savings bond.
Passports: gone.
Insurance: gone.
What remained was a single sheet of thick stationery, center-folded.
Lucas unfolded it.

Blank.
Completely.
But the paper held faint impressions of writing, as though someone had pressed hard on a prior page.
He angled it under the lamp.

Couldn't read the ghost letters, yet they were there—
the shadows of words stripped of ink.

Lucas felt unmoored, like a diver who reaches for a
safety rope and finds only water.

He replaced the paper, closed the safe, spun the dial to
scrambled numbers.

His breathing grew uneven—swift draughts of air, then
pauses that ached behind the sternum.
Training from his marathon days kicked in: count to four
on the inhale, hold for two, exhale eight.
It steadied him enough to think.

Next step?
He needed police to take him seriously.
Evidence beyond empty closets.
The card, the dead phone, the missing passports.
Would that suffice?

He pictured Officer Bauer—he knew many by name
because Julia taught a self-defense workshop for
precinct staff.
Bauer's patience would contract if Lucas barged in at
daybreak carrying only suspicion and a foreign bank
card.

He glanced at the wall clock.
06:37.
The station opened at eight.
He had eighty-three minutes to gather every anomaly.
To prove absence.
To quantify a void.

He walked briskly to the study where Julia's desktop computer sat.

The monitor showed a login prompt.

He typed her usual passphrase.

Denied.

He tried her alternate.

Denied.

Third time: denied; user locked out.

So either she changed it recently, or someone else had.

He moved to his own laptop.

Logged in.

Opened email.

Scanned sent messages for auto-forwards.

Nothing outward.

He opened the shared calendars.

Her upcoming appointments had vanished.

Blocks of color replaced by blank cells.

Even the reminder she had set for tonight's anniversary dinner at Cielo Verde was gone.

Lucas stared at the white space where intention used to be.

He checked cloud storage.

The folder labeled "Wedding_July-18" existed.

Inside, fifty photos previously curated as favorites were empty thumbnails—grey icons with a slash.

A prickling marched across his scalp.

The deletion felt like a careful erasure of shared history, but why some and not others?

Choosing what to leave behind shaped the story nearly as much as what was removed.

He closed the laptop with a muted click.

The apartment vibrated faintly as the building's boiler fired up, reminding tenants to wake, shower, fry eggs. Lucas felt decoupled from those mundane expectations.
Yet some muscle memory pushed him toward routine: he brewed coffee, not because he wanted the taste but because the aroma grounded him.
Steam coiled up, carrying notes of burnt caramel.

He sipped, throat tight, eyes on the window where dawn had completed its shift into day.
Pale clouds drifted like bandages across the sky. Somewhere in the city, Julia could be watching the same sky, coffee in hand, safe, intentional.
Or she could be underground, phone smashed, ring surrendered as a final symbol.

The thought nearly buckled him.
He steadied himself by gripping the counter's edge.

To quell spiraling speculation, he forced method:
—Search trash for clues.
—Collect phone records.
—Photograph every odd detail: ring, toothbrush, missing closets, bank card.
—Compile a timeline.

He fetched his DSLR from the bookshelf.
First shot: the ring glinting lonely on the coaster.
Second: the empty wardrobe.

Third: the toothbrush still erect beside his, color contrast stark.
Fourth: EC card in his palm, name crisp under macro lens.

With each click, the world felt marginally more contained, as though evidence formed a net that might keep him from falling through cognitive holes.

He poured the rest of the coffee down the sink—nausea had replaced appetite—and rinsed the mug.
Mechanics.
Keep moving.

Back in the bedroom, he knelt to slide the storage boxes fully into the open.
Tax files: he riffled through receipts, found nothing altered.
Polaroid box: images preserved nights in Barcelona, Prague, Vienna—all featured both of them, smiling, blurred, imperfect, alive.
He stacked the boxes aside, reached deeper, fingers sweeping.
Nothing else.
No second card, no note.

He returned to the closet, peered at the shelves.
Noticed a narrow envelope taped to the underside of the topmost plank—an angle he'd never naturally see.
Heart banging, he retrieved it.
Unsealed.
Inside: a single hotel brochure, folded to conceal its cover.

He opened.

Hotel Nebozízek, Prague.

A baroque building on Petřín Hill, view of Charles Bridge.

Room rates circled in blue pen.

No reservation confirmation, just the brochure.

Julia disliked brochures; she planned trips digitally.

But perhaps Karolina collected paper.

Lucas's mouth whispered the foreign name.

Karolina Vondráková.

He said it again, slower, feeling shape and rhythm.

It fit the geography of Prague.

Was she a friend?

An accomplice?

A target?

A fiction?

The heater clicked off; warm pipes ticking as metal cooled.

He realized the day had stepped fully into Saturday.

Their sixth anniversary morning without the woman who shaped half of every plan.

He reached for his phone again—still dead.

He removed the SIM and placed it into a spare handset kept for travel.

Screen lit.

Battery 100%.

So the SIM survived; the original hardware had been disabled.

Missed calls: none.

Texts: none.

Message history with Julia: the entire thread gone.
As if never existed.

He sank onto the edge of the bed, numb.
The ring on the table caught sunlight, throwing a tiny disk of gold against the wall.
A silent Morse code.

Lucas stood, slid the ring into its velvet box from the proposal.
He closed the lid gently, pocketed it alongside the foreign card.

Finally, he dressed: jeans, hoodie, windbreaker.
Wallet, passport (his own still present), camera bag, evidence pouch improvised from a freezer bag.
He slipped on shoes, hesitated, then added the hotel brochure.

Before exiting, he did a last sweep.
Heated towel rack silent.
The kitchen faucet off.
Lights extinguished one by one until only the hallway lamp remained.

He opened the apartment door.
Air in the corridor felt cooler, more objective, less intimate.
He locked the door behind him, testing the handle twice.
Pocketed the key.
Paused, listening for any sign of Julia's laughter, footfall, apology, explanation.
None came.

Lucas inhaled, shallow but steady, and walked toward the stairwell.
Each step downward sounded louder than physics allowed, like the building amplified his leaving.

At street level, the city yawned awake.
Bakery shutters rolled up.
A cyclist rattled past, earbuds tucked, unaware of the missing piece in Lucas's world.

He turned right, heading for the police precinct.
In his pocket, the ring nudged his thigh with each stride.
The card's edges bit soft reminder.
He fingered both, anchoring to these mute witnesses.

Somewhere ahead waited a desk sergeant primed to doubt him.
He rehearsed his report:
"My wife is gone.
She left behind her ring, her toothbrush, and possibly a borrowed identity."

It sounded fragile, but it was all he had.

Lucas lengthened his gait, breath clouding in the cool morning, heartbeat syncing to the cadence of urgency.
Behind him, six floors up, the apartment windows reflected sunrise like blind eyes.
Inside, the empty bed cooled further, a crater of absent warmth.

The day, indifferent, pressed on.
Lucas pressed back, one step after the last, carving a path toward answers—or deeper riddles.

He did not yet know that every question he asked would open two more.

Nor that the name Karolina Vondráková would echo louder than Julia's within forty-eight hours.

But he felt the vibration of fate under his soles, a subterranean train approaching a station with no posted schedule.

And he kept walking.

CHAPTER 2

PAPERLESS GHOST

Lucas waited in the blue-white precinct lobby, clutching the printed photo like a boarding pass to reality. Fluorescent lights hummed.

Cameras on the ceiling glimmered with quiet judgment. A poster behind the reception desk read *If You See Something, Say Something*—but what if the thing you saw left no shadow?

Officer Bauer emerged, mid-thirties, buzz cut, coffee in one hand, tablet in the other.

Lucas rose.

Bauer motioned him through turnstiles.

Interview Room Two: pastel walls, metal table, two molded chairs bolted to the floor.

Lucas handed over the photo:

Beach picnic, sunset, Julia leaning against him, wind in her hair, laughter frozen in pixels.

He had chosen this image because her eyes were bright, undeniable, alive.

Bauer scanned the print into the precinct database.

A progress bar crawled across the screen.

Lucas listened to it tick upward like a countdown to sanity.

Then a chime.

"Zero matches," Bauer read.

He tried a second filter, facial-recognition network tied to passports, licenses, immigration cards.

Again: no result.

Bauer frowned, clicked deeper.

"Name?"

"Julia Schwarz. Born twenty-ninth of April, 1989. Grew up in München, lived in Berlin four years, then here."

Bauer typed.

Database returned: *No record.*

Lucas tasted iron behind his teeth.

"Try maiden name, maybe Brüning."

Bauer tried.

"No record."

Middle name? Nickname? he asked.

Lucas shook his head.

Julia had once joked that her middle initial was *None*, so official that she wrote it with a capital N.

Bauer tapped the table with his stylus.

"Could be she uses a different legal name," he suggested, tone professional yet fraying at the edges.

He swiveled the screen so Lucas could see rows of empty fields, blank lines where identity should live.

"It happens," Bauer added.

"Not to my wife," Lucas whispered.

They finished the intake form.

Bauer promised to circulate the image to patrols but hinted resources were thin.

Lucas left fingerprints on the visitor signature pad before stepping back into the hallway.

The door thudded shut behind him, like a vault sealing out certainty.

Outside, early traffic pulsed past in ribbons of noise.
Lucas thumbed his phone—not the sabotaged original but the spare handset.
He pulled up WhatsApp.
Julia's chat bubble waited at the top of the list, still favorited with a red heart.
He opened it.

Blank.
No messages.
No photos.
No stickers.
Years of conversation—teasing, planning, mundane grocery notes—evaporated.
Only a single system line remained: *You created this group "Julia ❤" on 17 July 2020.*
Not even a goodbye.

Lucas backed out, scrolled older backups.
Google Drive snapshots appeared, each dated, but when tapped delivered only progress spinners that never resolved.
He pictured code running, finding zero-byte files where memory should be stored.
A digital shrug.

He screenshots the emptiness, saving proof of the vanishing.
Proof for whom?

He dialed Martin—best man at their wedding, college roommate, practiced skeptic.
Three rings, pickup.
"Hey Lu, everything okay?"
"Need to talk. About Julia."
"Julia who?" Martin sounded tired, maybe hung-over.
"Julia *my wife*."
Silence, then uneasy laughter.
"Buddy, you never brought a Julia to poker night. This another thriller project?"
Lucas's spine chilled.
"You toasted us at our wedding."
"Dude, I gave a toast at *your* wedding to—" pause, "—your book deal. No bride. We all joked you married the manuscript."
"Stop." Lucas's voice cracked.
Martin softened. "Look, if this is some immersive promo—"
Lucas ended the call.

He rang Clara, coworker, gym partner of Julia.
Clara answered on a treadmill, breathless.
When Lucas asked, her stride faltered.
"I've emailed with someone named Julia to schedule classes," she said. "But we never met."
Lucas pressed.
"Honestly, I thought she was you using a feminine

alias. Kind of cute."
He hung up before anger splashed over.

Call after call, similar notes:
—No friend recalled speaking to Julia in person.
—No video calls, only emails that read like Lucas's style.
—Photos existed, yes, but always *sent by Lucas*.

The calls ended when his battery grazed red.
He was left on a park bench, wind unsettled, as if the city exhaled secrets.

Afternoon.
He returned to the apartment, keys rattling like dice.
Inside, the rooms felt wider, emptier, as though Julia's absence had inflated the space.
He headed straight to her nightstand.

Top drawer: scented hand cream, bookmark, three unused earplugs, a coaster imprint where the water glass used to sit.
Lower drawer: journals with broken spines—he flipped pages.
Blank.
All volumes.
Paper that once absorbed ink now pristine.
He scraped a fingernail along a page, looking for indentations.
Smooth.

Wardrobe again—confirmed void.
He pulled out drawers, lifted false bottoms: no
passport, no medical card, no utility bills in her name.
He checked the safe once more; still only the ghost-
written stationery.
He tore it free, placed graphite over, shaded softly: faint
lines appeared, but unreadable; some letters looked
Slavic.

Kitchen drawer labeled *Health*: his insurance card; her
slot empty.
He dug further, found an envelope addressed to
Resident from the city clinic, dated six months back.
 Inside: appointment reminder for Lucas, none for Julia.

Bathroom cabinet—he lined toiletries on the counter.
His deodorant, his cologne, their shared first-aid kit.
But her prescription bottle absent.
She took thyroid medication nightly; now no orange
vial.
Evidence of bodily needs erased.

Lucas crouched, shoulders hitting tile, mind scrambling
for any physical artifact that she could not erase—
hairpins in the drain, DNA in the sheets.
But memory fought memory: had he ever unclogged
her hair from the shower?
Maybe she wore it up.
Maybe he just never noticed.

Panic slid into a slow-burning doubt.
Could he have constructed her, neuron by neuron?
Grief hallucination that lasted years, not moments?

He pressed fists to his temples.

No. Too many photos, too many tactile memories: her skin smelling of bergamot, her laugh with a cracked note on the inhale, the mole at the base of her neck shaped like a semicolon.

Yet every tangible proof lay in the realm of personal recall, intangible to the world.

He needed objective data.

He powered up his laptop.

Email account open.

Search for *from:Julia*, yielded empty.

He checked *sent* folder.

Hundreds of messages—editors, utilities, promotions—none to Julia.

But he remembered writing to her about dinner, vacations, those quick "miss you" notes.

Had he dream-typed?

He logged into the joint bank portal, rubbing the foreign EC card for luck.

Only his account showed; the joint savings account—gone.

Transaction history absent.

No mortgage payments with Julia's signature.

The ledger made him appear single.

He screenshotted everything, timestamped it.

A digital map of erasure.

Evening light slanted amber across the floor.
Lucas realized he had eaten nothing since before dawn.
The fridge had the soup.
He heated it, spoon shaking.
Swallowed two mouthfuls, gagged at the texture, dumped the rest.

He sat at the kitchen island, notebook open, created two columns:
Known Facts vs. **Missing.**

Facts:
—Wedding photos exist in personal possession.
—Neighbors saw Julia at least once (he thought).
—The ring.
—The toothbrush.
—Her signature scent bottle was here last week.

Missing:
—All official documentation.
—Institutional recognition.
—Witnesses who interacted with her independently.
—Digital footprints not traceable to Lucas's devices.

He chewed the pen cap, circled *neighbors*.
He needed external confirmation.

He left the apartment, rapped on the door opposite.
Mrs. Krause, retired chemist, answered in floral housecoat.
"Ah, Herr Lucas."
"Did you see Julia leave this morning?"
Mrs. Krause tilted her head.

"Who?"

"My wife."

"I thought you lived alone, dear. Except for that cat that visits your balcony."

Lucas thanked her vaguely, retreated.

Next, the floor above: an artist couple, Tobias and Rena.

Tobias answered holding a paint-stained rag.

"Julia?" he echoed. "Never met. Only you."

Rena emerged, shook her head.

They invited Lucas in for tea; he declined.

The stairwell felt cavernous.

He descended to the super's basement office.

Herr Holtz peered over bifocals.

"Yes, your wife," Holtz said slowly, "I believe I've seen her collecting packages—"

Lucas exhaled relief.

Holtz continued, tapping forehead.

"Now I think: perhaps that was you. Same height, maybe a hat?"

Relief snapped.

Lucas climbed back upstairs, legs heavy.

In the apartment again, he stared at the reflection in the balcony door.

His own face wavered against the darkening skyline.

He tried to overlay Julia's image beside his but the glass stayed solitary.

He fetched the DSLR, took a new photo of the
bedroom: just sheets, ring box, his solitary figure.
He reviewed the shot.
A tiny blot on the digital preview—maybe dust, maybe
something more—hovered where Julia once slept.
He zoomed.
Just pixel noise.

He thought of the half-filled Polaroids: both of them
present.
He rummaged for the shoebox, yanked it open.
Pulled a random Polaroid: picnic again, same as the
print, but in this copy Julia's face blurred past
recognition, an overexposed smear.
Second Polaroid: Christmas, tree lights; her body semi-
transparent, the ornaments behind shining through.
He fanned the stack.
Across them all, Julia decayed—washed-out, ghosted,
absent.
He hadn't noticed before, or maybe the corruption
spread only today.

Lucas's pulse drummed.
His laptop chimed: email received.
He opened.
Subject line: *Karolina Vondráková*.
No sender address.
Single attachment: JPEG.
He hesitated, then opened it.
A scanned passport page.
Female, brown hair, date of birth identical to Julia's.
Eyes green where Julia's were hazel.

Name: Karolina Vondráková.
Nationality: Czech.
Lucas compared the photo.
Hair longer but jawline familiar.
A sister image of Julia, shifted five degrees sideways.

Below the image, one sentence in Czech: *Nezapomeň, co jsi slíbil.*
He translated aloud from college Czech: "Don't forget what you promised."

Hands trembling, he saved the file, forwarded it to himself on a backup account.
He printed a copy for the evidence folder.

Night settled.
The apartment lost detail.
Lucas sat on the floor surrounded by artifacts: blurred Polaroids, ring box, toothbrush, foreign EC card, printed passport, graphite-ghost letter.
He arranged them in a circle, as if summoning context.
Inside the ring of clues, he forced himself to speak Julia's name, over and over, shaping it into the air like a mantra.
But the echo that came back felt thinner each time, as though language itself doubted the referent.

He slid the ring onto his palm, closed fingers around it until the metal's edge pressed a crescent into his skin.
Pain confirmed existence; but whose?

At 22:43 he called Bauer again, voicemail this time.
Left a message: "Evidence mounting. Need to report identity theft or worse. Please call."
He forgot to add his number; Bauer already had it.

Lucas lay on the couch, fully dressed, documents fanned across coffee table like tarot.
He tried to focus on factual anchors: the heat of her body once beside him, the cadence of her laugh, the night she said yes under fairy lights.
Memory fought decomposition.
He would not surrender her to absence without collision.

Finally, exhaustion drugged his eyelids.
Sleep came in staccato bursts.
Dreams placed him in empty rooms, calling a name that dissolved into static before reaching walls.

At 03:12 he woke, heart battering.
He checked the front door.
Bolted.
Then the bedroom.
Still empty.
He stood in the threshold, feeling for vibrations of another heartbeat.
Only the refrigerator's motor hummed downstream.

He whispered into the darkness:
"Julia, if you're real, find me.
If you're not, let me wake entirely."

No reply, save the muted tick of the hallway clock, each second erasing a sliver more of certainty.

Lucas remained upright until dawn etched the sky again, cradling the ring in one hand, the foreign card in the other, wondering which belonged to truth, which to delusion, and whether there was still a line between them at all.

CHAPTER 3

INVISIBLE INK

Lucas woke to the metallic scrape of the garbage truck below the window.

He had slept an hour, maybe two.

The ring still sat in his fist, imprinting a half-moon on his palm.

Outside, morning diluted the city into a gray wash.

He rose, showered, dressed in yesterday's jeans, yesterday's questions.

Herr Holtz unlocked his basement office at eight sharp.

Lucas was waiting in the corridor, a cardboard tray of coffees—peace offering.

Holtz adjusted his bifocals.

"Long night, Herr Lucas?"

Lucas nodded, handed him a cup.

"I need to ask again about Julia."

A pause, polite and heavy.

Holtz sipped.

"I said yesterday: I've never met a woman living with you."

Lucas leaned forward.

"We signed the lease together. You checked both

passports."

"I remember *you* signing," Holtz said.

His tone had shifted—no irritation, just firm distance, like a librarian correcting a misfiled book.

Lucas pulled out his phone, opened the gallery, showed a photo of Julia painting the balcony rail the week they moved in.

Holtz studied the screen, eyebrows knitting.

"This looks like our building, yes. But I don't recall seeing her."

Lucas bit back frustration.

"You brought her the extra flower box that day."

Holtz shook his head.

"I delivered it to you. Alone."

Lucas swallowed.

"Then let's watch the security feed."

Holtz hesitated, but curiosity won over.

He led Lucas into the tiny monitoring room—a cave of dusty monitors and the musk of solder and paper.

He keyed in a supervisor code.

Week-by-week thumbnails appeared.

They started with yesterday.

The entrance camera: Lucas enters with groceries.

No Julia.

Last month: Lucas drags a suitcase; camera shows him talking over his shoulder, gesturing to empty space.

No Julia.

Move-in day: a van, Lucas carrying boxes.

Behind him should have been Julia balancing a lamp.

The pixel space beside him was bare.

Minute after minute, Lucas watched himself perform a pantomime—doors held open, heads turned, lips moving to someone invisible.
Only once did a flicker of static distort the feed, and Holtz blamed the weather.

Lucas's hands trembled.
He felt exposed, like a man being told the mirror had never truly reflected him.
Holtz placed a paternal hand on his shoulder.
"Perhaps the lens angle missed her?"
All angles missed her, Lucas thought, because someone clipped her out.

He asked for copies of the files.
Holtz complied, burning them to a flash drive.
Lucas thanked him, voice scraping.

Trattoria Fiori, 13:00.
Lucas stepped inside, welcomed by oregano and simmering tomatoes.
They had celebrated promotions here, argued over wine here, flirted across checkered tablecloths here.
He spotted Sergio, the owner, polishing glasses.

"Buon pomeriggio, signore," Sergio greeted.
No recognition in his eyes beyond standard courtesy.
Lucas forced a smile.
"Table for two, please. Maybe the corner booth?"
Sergio scanned the near-empty dining room.
"All tables free. Sit where you like."

Lucas slid into their usual booth—third from the window, view of the street.

He waited.

He imagined Julia shrugging off her coat, ordering mineral water with lime, teasing him about over-tipping.

The waitress arrived.

Lucas leaned in.

"You remember my wife, Julia? Curly hair, hazel eyes. We eat here almost every Thursday."

The waitress looked politely blank.

"Sorry. I only started three months ago."

Lucas waved Sergio over.

The owner folded his hands on the edge of the table.

"You've been here before, certo," he said. "Always alone. Sometimes with manuscript pages."

Lucas stared.

"We held our anniversary here last July. You poured us limoncello on the house."

Sergio shook his head.

"I remember limoncello for you and the chef. No lady."

Lucas pulled out his phone, scrolling to a photo of him and Julia clinking glasses beneath the trattoria's mural.

The waitress peered.

"That looks like our wall for sure," she said, "but it's only you. The other half is… empty?"

Lucas zoomed.

Julia's silhouette had faded into ghost blur—colors bleeding into the background.

He gasped.

Sergio offered a gentle squeeze of the shoulder, an apology without words.

Lucas left without ordering, appetite drowned in static.

He hurried to **Berliner Sparkasse**, where the safe-deposit vault yawned cold behind layers of steel.
An attendant escorted him to cubicle 4-B.
Lucas twisted the key, lifted the lid.

Inside:—Property deeds.—University diploma.
 —Birth certificate.
 But the cream envelope stamped *Standesamt*—their marriage certificate—was gone.

He rifled through files, careful yet frenzied, like searching pockets for a life-saving pill.
Narrow cedar scent filled the booth.
No certificate.

Back at the counter, he demanded the staff check the log.
The clerk clicked through timestamps.
Box accessed eight days earlier.
Signature: Lucas Schwarz.
A digital pen stroke identical to his own.
But he had not been here in months.

He left with a new void where legal proof once rested.

Late afternoon, Lucas marched into **Charité-Mitte Medical Records**, adrenaline pleading for answers.

Receptionist asked for ID.

He presented his passport; the system retrieved his file.

"Do you want the full printout or just the summary?" she asked.

"Full," Lucas said, pulse pounding.

She returned with a thick envelope.

Lucas thanked her, found an empty hallway bench, and opened the accordion folds.

It started normally: childhood immunizations, broken arm age nine, wisdom teeth extraction.

Then a new section dated four years back—*Psychiatric & Cognitive Disorders*.

Diagnosis: **Schizoaffective Disorder, Dissociative Subtype**.

Treating physician: Dr. Ernst Mayer.

Prescription history: antipsychotics, mood stabilizers, monthly therapy sessions.

Lucas felt the building tilt.

He had never met Dr. Mayer.

He had never swallowed those pills.

He scanned for signature lines—his own scribbled consent, allegedly, on every form.

The handwriting could have passed for his under duress.

After each renewal, a note: *Patient continues to experience delusional partner syndrome. Hallucinated spouse "Julia."*

Lucas's stomach lurched.

Blood roared in his ears.

A nurse passing by paused.

"Sir? Need water?"

He nodded.

She guided him to a chair, brought a paper cup.

Hand trembling, he searched online for Dr. Ernst Mayer.

Clinic address existed, phone number rang, but the website looked newly built—stock photos, generic copy.

He called; an automated voice requested he leave a message.

Lucas folded the records back into the envelope like evidence from a crime scene.

He left the hospital, winter sun a white blade across his vision.

Back home, the apartment felt staged, props rearranged.

The DSLR lay on the coffee table where he'd left it.

He powered it, pointed it at the hallway mirror, snapped a photo, reviewed.

His reflection alone, of course.

But behind him, near the bedroom door, a faint whorl of pixels—like steam dissipating.

He leaned closer.

Could be glare.

Could be her.

Lucas set the camera on continuous mode, placed it on a tripod facing the living room, and let it click every five seconds.

Meanwhile he opened the flash drive from Holtz.

He scrubbed through footage again, frame by frame, seeking any glitch, any hint of Julia's outline.

Nothing.

He opened his laptop to a blank document and wrote:

1. *Caretaker denies.*

2. *Cameras deny.*

3. *Restaurant denies.*

4. *Marriage cert missing.*

5. *Medical file rewritten.*

Underneath he scrawled a question: *How does one prove a person who might be memory only?*

He saved it as *Proof_of_Julias_Existence.docx*—the filename itself felt desperate.

He called the civil registry, requesting a copy of the marriage license.

The clerk entered his ID data, paused.

"No record under that registry office," she said.

Lucas insisted.

She searched variations.

Nothing.

"Do you perhaps have the document number?"

It had vanished with the certificate.

He hung up, feeling a cold corridor open inside him.

Next, he rang his mother in Munich.
She answered in bright Bavarian tone.
"Alles gut, Luci?"
"Do you remember meeting Julia?"
A hesitation layered with worry.
"You spoke of a girlfriend once, but we never met. You cancelled the Christmas visit saying she was ill."
Lucas's mind flashed to that December—Julia down with flu, heavy snow.
"We video-called," he protested.
Mother sounded uneasy.
"We talked on FaceTime, just you, darling."

Lucas ended the call gently, hands damp with perspiration.

The camera's memory card finished.
He reviewed the hundred frames.
Across thirty minutes, his apartment remained static: couch, plant, painting.
On frame eighty-three, the hallway light flickered.
A blur—vertical smear about human height—across the doorway.
Next frame, gone.

Lucas magnified the blur—periphery of a face?
Or motion artefact?
He increased contrast; lines sharpened into uncertainty.

He saved the best still, titled it *PossibleJulia.jpg*.
He printed it, pinned it to the wall above his desk,

beside the foreign EC card and the passport scan and the empty WhatsApp screenshots.

A fever board built from silence.

He sat back, eyes burning, trying to breathe through the sense of being outnumbered by shadows.

At 23:10 his phone rang.

No caller ID.

He answered.

A low female voice spoke in accented German.

"Lucas, you promised."

Heartbeat hammered.

"Julia?"

A faint exhale.

"No names. They listen."

"Where are you?"

"Where you began."

"What does that mean?"

Click.

Silence.

He replayed the call in his mind.

Where you began.

They met in Prague on a research trip.

Hotel Nebozízek—a hill above the city, apple trees in bloom.

Could she be there?

Or was *they* the doctors? The system rewriting his life?

He packed a small backpack: passport, cash, camera, laptop, ring, EC card, medical file copy, clothes.

He booked a train on his phone—Berlin to Prague,
early morning.
Confirmation code popped up, glowing like a lifeline.

Before sleeping, he glanced again at the pinboard.
So many pieces, none fitting.
Yet the shape looked increasingly like a doorway.

He set an alarm for 04:30, collapsed onto the couch,
but sleep refused.
Memories replayed: Julia's laugh in the trattoria, her
sigh of delight at lake reflections, her weight beside him
in bed.
Were those senses reliable or stitched from longing?
He clenched his fist until nails bit flesh.
Pain felt real.
Therefore at least the one who *felt* must be real.

At 02:07, the hallway floor creaked.
Lucas sat upright.
"Julia?"
A faint click—camera shutter still on timer.
He stood, heart bouncing.
No one visible.
He fetched the camera, reviewed the latest frame:
living room dim, his silhouette, and to the left, by the
balcony door, a figure-shaped void in the darkness,
edges shimmering.
He whispered her name; darkness answered with
refrigerator hum.

03:59, he left the apartment.
Suitcase wheels whispered across the corridor carpet.
He did not lock the door; nothing left to guard.
The elevator descended, mirrored walls reflecting a man and his doubt.

Streetlights fizzed overhead.
He reached the Hauptbahnhof, neon buzz, 24-hour bakery.
Bought black coffee that tasted of burnt hope.
Boarded the train.
Found a window seat.
The carriage smelled of disinfectant and stale brioche.
He opened his notebook, wrote seven words: *If she is memory, I must remember.*

The train lurched.
Berlin slid backward, a tableau of lights dissolving.
Lucas felt both hunted and rescuer, victim and witness.
He pressed a hand to the glass.
Its chill steadied him.

He closed his eyes, let the rhythm of tracks drum lullabies of uncertainty.
Somewhere ahead, Prague waited, and with it either the woman he loved or the explanation for why the world insisted she had never breathed.

Behind him, the city erased footprints.

CHAPTER 4

RITUALS

The train rocked Lucas into a half-dream, rails humming beneath his skull.
He tried to rest, but memory would not stay quiet.
It peeled itself open, showing slivers of Julia he had missed while living beside her.

She always counted before sleep.
Not sheep, not seconds on a digital clock—she counted aloud in a whisper so faint he thought at first it was the radiator.
One, three, five, eight… always the same uneven ladder up to thirty-four, then silence.
If he spoke during the ritual, she would pause, inhale, start over.
He asked once why.
"Because some gaps can't be left empty," she murmured, then kissed him to stop the questions.

Photos unsettled her even on bright days.
At tourist spots she waited until strangers drifted away.
If someone lifted a phone too near, she stepped aside, turning her face to stone.
In cafés she chose the seat with her back to a wall and watched reflections in spoons.
Lucas teased her gently—"Camera-shy superstar?"—

but she only smiled, that tight smile that looked like it was sewn at the corners.

At home any snapshot that caught her unprepared was reviewed under hard light.

She examined pixels as if searching for a leak.

More than once Lucas found a newly printed photo sliced into ribbons in the trash, its edges curled like shed skin.

She dodged every question about family.

No stories of childhood summers, no aunties who baked too-sweet strudel, no lists of cousins.

If pressed, she sketched a vague village "near the mountains," a mother who "liked silence," a father "gone early."

Then she pivoted, asked Lucas about his parents, his thesis, his training runs—anything to move the beam off her.

One night, late October, wind rattling the casement, he woke to her crying on the bedroom floor.

She sat with knees up, forehead pressed to the mattress, shoulders shaking without sound.

He slid down beside her, draping his arm over her back.

Her spine felt brittle, as if every sob might snap a rib.

"I have to leave soon," she whispered.

"Why?"

"If I stay, it becomes… irreversible."

He tried to lift her face, but she kept it hidden.

After minutes that felt like hours she climbed back into

bed, cold as quarry stone, and counted the tremors of
his heartbeat until dawn.

She never joined his company gatherings.
There were invitations, name badges printed, extra
chairs reserved.
Something always intervened: a migraine, a project, a
last-minute trip.
Colleagues teased Lucas about his "mystery wife,"
thought she was an imaginary muse fueling his
manuscripts.
He laughed along, even when the joke stung.
Julia said crowds made her skin buzz, said he shouldn't
waste worry on small talk she'd only sabotage.
He let it pass, told himself privacy was her right.

Now, as Prague's suburbs blurred across the window,
the accumulations clanged together, forming a chain
he'd never felt tighten until it had cinched his throat.

The train hissed into Hlavní nádraží.
Lucas disembarked, backpack strapped tight, shards of
recollection rattling inside.
Station air smelled of diesel, pastry, disinfectant.
He followed tiled corridors to the luggage storage,
rented a locker for nothing but hours of past.

Outside, morning clogged the sky with low cloud.
He walked streets slick with last night's rain, eyes
scanning crowds for a profile he knew by heart.
But every woman was both Julia and not Julia, as if his
brain had given her face to the city in exchange for
answers.

Hotel Nebozízek sat halfway up Petřín Hill, reachable by the funicular Julia had loved.

He hiked instead, lungs burning, memories nipping at his heels.

At the summit he found the hotel's wrought-iron gate locked; renovation signs covered the windows.

He circled the building.

Graffiti marred one shutter: **KV 04/24** in looping blue paint.

Initials like a signature.

Karolina Vondráková?

A date two months past.

The mark felt fresh, possessive.

Lucas snapped a photo, heart quickening.

He pressed his palm to the cold metal, half expecting it to pulse back.

Nothing.

Just steel under an absent sun.

He descended the hill, mind tunneling into darker memory.

At the base, tourist stalls sold magnets and snow globes.

He bought nothing.

Hands jammed in pockets, fingers worrying the ring and the EC card like worry stones.

A café caught his eye—arched windows, lace curtains.

Name: **Kavárna Ticho**.

Silence Café.

He entered, soothed by muted clatter.

Ordered černá káva, took a corner table.

While the cup steamed he unfolded an envelope he had found wedged behind their apartment bookshelf before leaving Berlin—a stash of trip receipts and ticket stubs.
Among them was an old snapshot he didn't remember printing.

The photo showed a summer street market, stalls striped red and white, sunlight hammering down.
In the foreground Lucas haggled over peaches, head turned in mid-laugh.
Behind him, slightly out of focus, stood a woman looking straight at the lens.
Hair raven-dark, longer than Julia's habitual bob, wearing cat-eye sunglasses and a linen dress.
A cheap felt hat shaded her features, but the smile was unmistakable: Julia's mouth, the way it tilted left before rising.
Pinned to the dress was a vendor badge labeled **"VONDRÁKOVÁ, K."**

Lucas traced the outline on the glossy surface.
The timestamp printed by his camera read *17-07-2019*—two months before they met, or thought they met, in Prague.
Julia had always claimed to hate peaches.

He turned the photo over.
No annotation.
Just speckles where adhesive once held it in a notebook.
He stared until the inked date blurred.
When vision cleared, doubt had grown teeth.

A waitress refilled his water.

Lucas asked, voice low, if she recognized the woman in the photograph.

The waitress adjusted her glasses, squinted.

"Looks like a vendor from the farmers' market in Žižkov. Many girls work there in summer."

"Do you know her name?"

The waitress shrugged.

"A lot of students earn cash that way."

Lucas tapped the badge on the photo.

"That name? Vondráková?"

"Common surname," she said, apologetic.

Lucas thanked her, pocketed the photo, swallowed cold coffee.

Streetcars rattled past outside, their overhead lines sparking.

He felt as if his nerves had been wired into them, current crackling every time he blinked.

He pulled out his phone, opened the browser, searched Czech social networks for *Karolina Vondráková* paired with *Prague Market* and *Peaches*.

Thousands of hits.

He filtered: images.

Scroll after scroll: wedding guests, corporate headshots, teenagers with puppies.

Faces blurred together until he closed the tab to keep from drowning.

Memory kept poking.

The counting.

Had the sequence been Fibonacci?

1, 1, 2, 3, 5, 8, 13…

Yes.

She always paused after 13, whispered "Twenty-one"
like a confession, then finished at 34.

A mathematician's lullaby.

Why those numbers?

Growth patterns? Hiding spots?

He typed them into search: Fibonacci protection rituals.

Esoteric forums whispered about veils, about stepping
between frames of reality.

He scoffed, yet his pulse quickened like prey glimpsing
a predator in the grass.

His phone buzzed—a new email.

Sender: **unknown@oblivion.cz**

Subject: *You are close.*

No body, only an attachment: **IMG_0407.jpg**

He hesitated, then opened.

The image: a surveillance still of him in the café at this
very moment, head bent over the phone.

Time stamp: ten seconds ago.

Across the table, empty chair.

In the reflective window behind, a shape—slim,
feminine, hair pulled back—blurred by motion.

Julia?

Or someone wearing her echo?

He jerked his head up, scanning.

Café patrons stared at screens, pastries, nothing.

The waitress wiped a table.

Nobody looked rushed, nobody aimed a camera.
Yet someone watched.

Lucas left money, stepped outside, heel of his shoe
tapping cobblestone like a telegraph.
He spotted a narrow alley and ducked in, back pressed
to damp stone, breathing hard.
He replayed the night of her whispered warning: *before
it's too late*.
Too late for what?
For him to forget her?
For the world to sand her from every surface?
Perhaps the erasure accelerated with each memory he
clung to, like a program overwriting sectors the moment
they were accessed.

He needed a place the deletion couldn't reach, a
pocket of time unindexed.
Libraries, old archives—places still more paper than
pixel.
He remembered the **Klementinum**, Prague's baroque
library.
If Julia or Karolina left ink, maybe it waited there,
stubborn as dust.

He walked, pace sharpening.
Tourists clogged Karlův most, selfie sticks stabbing the
air.
He tucked his chin, sliding between groups.
His phone pinged again—another email, same sender:
Don't.
He silenced notifications, removed the battery for good

measure.

Analog from now on.

The Klementinum courtyard echoed with footsteps and pigeons.

Lucas approached the information desk, requested archival access.

The clerk produced a form.

Surname? First? ID?

He filled lines with stiff fingers, adding Julia's name under *Subject of research*.

The clerk led him through vaulted halls to a reading room lined with wooden cases.

A hushed cathedral smell: vellum, leather, time.

Lucas asked for newspapers July 2019, Prague-region human-interest.

He rolled reels on a microfilm viewer, images flicking past like moth wings.

Page after page of summer markets, charity fairs, photo essays.

On the third roll he froze: an article titled **"Farm-to-City Festival Draws Record Crowd."**

Center photo: stall of peaches, vendor wearing cat-eye sunglasses, linen dress, the badge **VONDRÁKOVÁ, K.**

Face clearer than his snapshot.

He printed the frame, pocketed it.

He searched for follow-up pieces.

A week later, a small column: **Karolina V. reported missing after festival.**

Police quote: "Left belongings at rented apartment, no signs of struggle."

Case unresolved.
He printed that too.

Lucas leaned back, mind spinning.
If Karolina vanished 2019, and Julia appeared 2020,
was Julia a new skin over the same person?
Or did she step into the hole Karolina left, wearing his
memories to keep from fading?

The counting ritual clicked—each Fibonacci number the
sum of the two before, a progression building on what
had vanished.
Carry only what can be generated from what remains.
An algorithm for existence.

He gathered prints, thanked the clerk, exited into late
afternoon light heavy as brass.
Clouds cracked; rain spotted the pavement.
He tucked the papers under his jacket, hurried toward
the river.

On a low stone wall he paused, breath fogging.
He unfolded the missing-person column, read it again.
Her photo stared back—same eyes, different hair,
different life.
He compared it with their honeymoon Polaroid (which
now, in memory, showed only him).
Two timelines, one face.
He tried to picture Karolina and Julia meeting in a
mirrored room, exchanging belongings like smugglers.
Which one cried on his bedroom floor?
Which one wrote her name in steam on the bathroom
mirror only to wipe it off before he noticed?

Thunder rumbled.

He ducked beneath a plane tree, shuffled papers into the backpack.

He fished out the ring box.

Opened it.

The band shone dull in the gray light.

Inside the band an inscription he had chosen: **L + J, 18-07-20**.

Date of a wedding no one recalled.

He wondered if the engraving would erode next.

Would the steel forget?

He snapped the box shut.

He needed allies—someone who knew him before the reshaping.

Perhaps the journalist who wrote Karolina's missing report.

Byline: **Petra Černá**.

He pulled a pen, scribbled her name on his wrist.

Ink bled in the drizzle, but stayed legible.

Streetlights flickered awake.

He retraced steps toward the hostel where he booked a bed.

In his room he pinned the new clippings beside the blurry still of café glass, forming a timeline:

2019 summer: Karolina Vondráková sells peaches. Vanishes.

2020 spring: Lucas meets Julia on Petřín Hill.

2025: Julia erased. Lucas diagnosed.

He stared until lines swam.
Sleep tugged with cold hands, yet he feared counts he could not complete.
He set the camera on the windowsill facing the narrow road, timer primed.
If something visited, he wanted evidence before it dissolved.

He lay on the bunk, backpack as pillow, counting backward this time—thirty-four, twenty-one, thirteen, eight, five, three, two, one—trying to understand what vanished in each subtraction.

Outside, rain played soft percussion on gutters.
Inside, the shutter clicked every five seconds, measuring absence in frames.

Lucas closed his eyes.
Behind them, he saw Julia at the edge of a photograph, reaching out as if to pull him through the paper into whatever place numbers could not locate.

He whispered her name once, let it hover in the dark.
Then sleep claimed him, leaving the room lit only by the blinking red eye of the camera, recording proofs that might still be there come morning—or might, like her, dissolve to nothing but static where a life had been.

CHAPTER 5

THREADS

Lucas woke beneath a ceiling of peeling plaster alive with foreign dreams.
A dorm-mate half–whispered through headphones, the hostel's pipes clanged, distant trams scraped the street.
He tasted copper on his tongue—leftover panic from the night.

The camera's memory card lay on the pillow like an unsent message.
He had no courage to check fresh frames; proof could wait.
His focus narrowed to a single name thrumming in his skull: **Karolina Vondráková**.

He dressed, slipped into drizzle, found a café that promised fast Wi-Fi and privacy.
The city lurched past outside—umbrellas blooming, cobbles shining.
Inside, a cracked-vinyl booth held him like confession.

Laptop open.
Browser awake.
He typed the name again, adding stray keywords—
Prague au pair, *missing student*, *host family dispute*.

Search engines shrugged; recent algorithms were polished mirrors, reflecting only what was already luminous.

He needed dustier glass.

So he tunneled down a staircase of hyperlinks into the sub-basements of the net: archived bulletin boards, abandoned listservs, forums still coded in green on black.

One corner—the migration-workers board—flickered to life after a twenty-second load.

Threads dated five, seven, ten years back.

He scrolled.

There: a post header *"AU PAIR GONE MISSING — PLEASE HELP"* dated August 2018.

Click.

Body text plain, frantic:

"My daughter Karolina, 23, was working for a family in Prague 2. Last seen after a quarrel with the father. Police slow. Please share her photo."

Below, an inline JPEG.

He clicked.

The image opened grainy, but her face punched through: Julia's cheekbones, Julia's steady eyes, hair longer, dyed a shade lighter.

Same smile with the ghost of an apology.

He stared until the edges blurred.

Friend replies trailed beneath—sympathy, theories, dead ends.

Thread ended cold.

At the bottom, a note: *Contact:*
Lenka.Vondrakova@centrum.cz
Lucas copied the address into a new mail, fingers
stumbling.
Subject: *Information about Karolina — URGENT.*
He typed, deleted, retyped, settled on: *"Please, I may*
have seen your daughter. Can we talk by phone?"
Sent.

Minutes stretched, measured by espresso sips.
Rain hardened outside, drumming windows.
Then: inbox ping.
Reply single line: *"Yes. Number below. I am here."*

Lucas dialed.
Tone rang across borders and years.
A woman answered on the second beat, voice frayed
by sleepless seasons.
"Yes?"

"Mrs. Vondráková? My name is Lucas Schwarz. I—"
He realized there was no gentle entrance.
"I believe I know your daughter. She may be using the
name Julia."

Silence ballooned, filled with static and breath.
Then a gasp.
"You've seen her? Alive?"

"I lived with her. I think I married her."
The words felt absurd in open air.
"Describe her," the mother whispered.

He painted features: hazel eyes that tipped toward
green in sunlight, a scar near the left eyebrow, laugh

with a cracked note.

At the second detail, the woman sobbed once, sharp.

"That is my Kája."

Lucas closed his eyes, throat tight.

"Where are you?" she asked.

"Prague. Searching."

She inhaled, long, as if drawing courage through the line.

"She told me once she might come back with a new face. I did not understand."

Voice cracked.

"Tell me everything, please."

Lucas outlined months of love and ordinary mornings, the sudden disappearance, the erasures, the diagnoses that smelled of fraud.

As he spoke, Mrs. Vondráková's breathing steadied, grief shifting to a practiced ledger of facts.

"She vanished in 2018," the mother said.

"Her agency placed her with a wealthy family—Veselý, district two.

The father—Marek.

Karolina wrote cheerful messages at first.

Then came a call, midnight.

She sounded frightened.

Said Marek had *plans*, that she found documents not meant for her.

Next day she was gone.

Police filed her as a runaway."

Lucas pictured Julia rifling locked drawers, that precise fear in her eyes whenever a camera dared catch her.

"Did she ever talk about using other names?" he asked.

The mother exhaled a shaky yes.
"Before Prague she worked in Italy under *Chiara Rossi*.
In Vienna as *Maria Leitner*.
Said it made travel easier.
I thought it youthful adventure."

Multiple skins.
A serpentine path.
Lucas felt the mosaic clicking into place yet leaving holes—who supplied these identities? And why did she keep catching fire and running?

The mother's voice dropped to a confession.
"I hired a private detective. He followed leads.
Said there was a pattern: families with power, men with secrets.
Karolina would grow close to the children, then disappear after a confrontation with the father."

Lucas shivered though the café steamed with heat.
"Did she mention numbers? Counting?"

The mother went quiet, then:
"Fibonacci. She used it as a game with my grandson when he was small. She said the sequence can grow forever, slipping between spaces."

Lucas's heartbeat drummed that spiral.
He asked for any remaining belongings of Karolina's.
The mother promised to scan photos, journals, mail

them tonight.

She thanked him in Czech, German, English, then the line went soft with her tears.

Lucas sat, phone limp in hand, staring at a café mural now humming with unseen stories.

He replayed the call, each syllable a weight.

The image of Julia-Karolina crying on his bedroom floor sharpened: she wasn't running from him, she was running from a loop that kept finding her.

He opened the thread again, browsed adjacent posts.

One user, handle *ClockworkFox*, claimed to have seen Karolina at a Prague night club weeks after her disappearance, hair chopped, calling herself *Eliska*.

Another pointed to a rumor—host father indicted on embezzlement charges but case vanished.

Lucas jotted notes.

He needed that father's full name: Marek Veselý.

He googled.

An article pay-walled.

He paid.

Headline from 2019: *"Tech Entrepreneur Cleared of Wrongdoing in Domestic Scandal."*

Content light, as if scrubbed.

No mention of an au pair.

Only a single photograph: Marek outside a courthouse, jaw tight.

Behind him, blurred figure of a woman turning away, face unrecognizable.

Lucas zoomed.

Hairline, posture, maybe—Julia.

But like every photo, details dissolved the closer he looked, as though pixels obeyed some higher censor.

He saved the file anyway.

The room felt smaller, oxygen thinning.
He closed the laptop, paid the bill, stepped into mid-afternoon rain.
Drops hit like Morse, querying his resolve.
He answered by moving.

He followed tram tracks toward Vinohrady, where upscale houses perched behind wrought-iron fences.
According to a dated address scrounged from the court docket, Veselý once lived on **Máchova 14**.
Lucas reached the gate: new name on the buzzer, renovation dust on windows.
Veselý had moved.
But neighbors remembered.

An elderly man watering geraniums eyed Lucas's photo.
"Ah, that nanny," he said in Czech-laced English.
"Pretty girl. One day police everywhere. Family gone soon after."
Any forwarding address?
Shrug.
"Rich people vanish better than ghosts."

Lucas thanked him, retreated.
He needed documents—legal, medical, whatever linked Karolina to that household.
Maybe the detective hired by Lenka kept files.
He messaged the mother again, requesting contact.

While waiting, he ducked into a laundromat, warmth spinning through machines.

He unlocked the camera at last, skimming last night's hostel frames.

Mostly static room, twitching curtains.

Frame 47: a blur by the door, shape of a woman half-formed in lamplight, then gone next frame.

He zoomed; the blur sharpened into nothing he could swear by.

Yet hope flickered—she lingered near.

Phone vibrated: email from Lenka with a PDF bundle—scans from the detective.

Lucas downloaded, heart hammering.

Eye-bleary pages loaded: pay slips to *K. Vondráková*, photocopies of visas under alternate names, a Czech police intake note describing recovered suitcase contents.

He scrolled, stopped.

Inventory listed: *Passport — name: Júlia Schwarz, issued Berlin 2019.*

Dated months *before* Lucas and Julia first spoke.

She had pre-forged their future.

Beneath, scribbled handwriting, detective's deduction: *Subject may create identities in advance, embedding into social nets before appearance.*

Lucas's stomach flipped.

She had orchestrated their meeting.

Had targeted him, or sheltered behind him?

He closed the PDF, palms sweating.
Hostel bed beckoned, but he feared sleep.
Instead he caught a tram toward Žižkov farmers'
market grounds, hoping old vendors remembered a girl
selling peaches.

The stalls were shuttered this late, canvas damp.
He walked the perimeter, imagining her laughter
echoing down the rows.
Rain pooled in drains, reflecting neon signs.
He leaned against a post, exhaustion clawing.

Lightning cracked distant and his phone lit—a call from
withheld number.
He answered.
A male voice: smooth, practiced.
"Mr. Schwarz," it said in accented German.
"You are asking many questions about someone who
prefers the past silent."
Lucas tightened grip.
"Who are you?"
"Friend. Consider this courtesy. Go back to Berlin.
Forget the girl."
"Why?"
"She lives longer when forgotten."
The line died.

Lucas stood in rain thickening to sheets.
He breathed the metallic scent, tasted decision.
Someone else hunted her, or caged her.
He wouldn't retreat.

He returned to hostel, used shaky Wi-Fi to search for Marek Veselý's newer companies.
One address popped—shared workspace near Karlín. Open tomorrow.
He planned, scribbled, set alarms.

Before turning off the light, he opened the scanned photo again—the market, the badge, the smile.
He whispered, "Karolina, Julia, whoever you are, hold on."
Outside, trams clicked like distant camera shutters counting down.

Sleep came ragged, stitched with images: Julia multiplying in mirrors, each version shedding a name like burning paper, Lucas chasing but the hallway stretched, numbers floating overhead—1, 2, 3, 5, 8... until they blurred into static.

He woke before dawn, pulse uneven yet determined.
Today he would face the man whose life intersected hers with violence.
Today he would pry another tile from the mosaic.

As he packed the backpack he slipped the peach-market photo into his jacket pocket, a compass of sorts.
He glanced at the camera—battery charged, memory card emptied to laptop.
Evidence secured.

Outside, the sky cracked pink along the horizon; Prague slowly revealed its scars.
Lucas stepped into the chill, counting under his breath—

One.

Two.

Three.

Five.

Eight—

Not stopping until he felt her presence riding the rising Fibonacci like a rope he could climb through whatever hole she'd fallen into years ago.

CHAPTER 6

SILHOUETTES

Dawn smudged gray onto Prague's rooftops as Lucas crossed the hostel corridor toward the shared showers, towel over his shoulder, resolve in his chest.
Half-asleep travelers shuffled by.
His phone vibrated—unknown number, Czech prefix.
He almost let it slide to voicemail; instead he answered.

A man spoke fluent German edged with Viennese consonants.
"You're looking for the woman with changing names."
Lucas stopped walking.
"Yes. Who is this?"
A soft, humorless laugh.
"Someone who spent three years forgetting her and failed."
Lucas felt the hallway shrink.
"What do you want?"
"To trade nightmares for facts. Café Na Hraně, Žitná Street, back room, one hour."
Before Lucas could agree, the call ended.

He dressed fast—black sweater, jacket, backpack with his growing archive.
Outside, drizzle sifted through weak sunlight.
Traffic hissed past.

He walked, counting silently, anchoring nerves to the Fibonacci rhythm: one, two, three, five, eight…

Café Na Hraně lived up to its name—On the Edge. Graffiti crept to its second-floor windows; interior smelled of strong roast and damp books.
A barista nodded Lucas toward a curtain-separated alcove.

Inside waited a man early forties, thin, hairline retreating, eyes rimmed by nights without mercy.
He rose, hand extended.
"Anton Weiss."
Lucas shook it.
"Lucas Schwarz."
They sat across a wobbling table.
Between them lay a canvas messenger bag bulging with paper.

Anton's voice carried two speeds—quick when facts lined up, slower when memory drew blood.
"I knew her as Sophie Berger," he began.
"We met in Vienna. 2017. She worked at a language school, said she was half-Swiss, half-French."
He slid a photo forward: winter market, lights strung overhead, a woman balanced on skates, scarf whipped around her mouth.
Julia's eyes looked out, amused, cautious.

Lucas touched the print.
The image held—no blur, no erasure—yet its permanence felt temporary, like ink still drying.
"She hated photos," Lucas murmured.

Anton nodded.

"I had to beg for every shot. She let me keep six."

He fanned them: Sophie riding a rented bike, Sophie feeding swans, Sophie asleep on a train seat—each angle intimate, each smile wary.

Lucas's pulse stuttered between awe and dread.

Anton produced plastic sleeves stuffed with ticket stubs, birthday cards, emails printed in color.

Correspondence read like Julia's cadence—short lines, lowercase i's, foreign spell-check betrayals.

Sophie joked about the Fibonacci series, signing off *34 kisses*.

Lucas felt sweat bead on his neck.

"She told me her parents were dead," Anton said.

"She called them ghosts."

His fingers trembled; he clasped them.

"Then one night she vanished. Apartment emptied, toothbrush left."

Lucas exhaled—an echo of his own story.

Anton leaned forward, blue irises gleaming like cracked glass.

"I reported her missing. Police found no record of a Sophie Berger. My friends swore I'd invented her."

He swallowed.

"I kept digging. That got me fourteen days in a psychiatric wing near Währing."

"On what grounds?"

"Paranoid delusions. They said I showed classic signs—confabulated lover, conspiracy about erased

evidence. My employer signed the paperwork."
Lucas's stomach turned.
Same path laid for him.

Anton traced a coffee stain on the table.
"They dosed me—olanzapine, diazepam. I drooled
through therapy while they told me to let go of my
imaginary fiancée."
He stared at Lucas with exhausted triumph.
"I never did."

Lucas placed his own prints on the table: the peach-
market photo, the surveillance still from Kavárna Ticho,
the blurred hostel frame.
Anton studied them, jaw taut.
"That's Sophie. Longer hair, different clothes, but that's
her."
He tapped the peach picture.
"She wore that hat in Florence. Said it made her feel
invisible."

They sat amid clatter of cups, voices muffled by walls.
Lucas asked, "Did she mention a host family? A man
named Marek Veselý?"
Anton shook his head.
"She avoided specifics. But she talked about men who
thought they owned the world. Said she'd borrowed
things they didn't deserve."
He hesitated.
"Sometimes she'd wake screaming. Not nightmares—
strategies. She'd whisper sequences, times, train
numbers, repeating them until the panic drained."

Lucas pictured Julia at his bedside counting.
A code, not a quirk.

Anton unzipped the bag again, withdrew a slim notebook.
"I found this under floorboards after she left. I don't read Czech, but maybe you can decode."
Lucas opened to dense columns of digits—date stamps paired with station abbreviations, then names: *Milan*, *Zurich*, *Berlin*, all scrawled beside looping arrows.
On several pages the word *SOMA* appeared, circled.
Lucas tasted metal—Greek for body, Sanskrit for moon, brand name for muscle relaxant.
Or a codename.

Anton watched him read.
"Since the clinic, I live off contract work, keep moving. Every six months I search her latest alias forums. That's how I found your posts."
Lucas frowned.
"I never posted."
Anton shrugged.
"Photos of you looking for Julia surfaced on a darknet board last night. Someone's tracking you."

Lucas recalled the email attachments—the café still— someone already inches from his shadow.

Anton leaned in, voice dropping to a hiss.
"I learned the pattern. She enters a life, stays until a line is crossed—money, abuse, secrets—then slips skin, becomes new. Anyone who tangles with her risks being blanked. Not killed, erased."

He rubbed the back of his wrist where a hospital band had once lived.

"They rewrite you until even your mother doubts you."

Lucas's breath fogged the tabletop.

"But why me? Why marry?"

Anton's look softened.

"Maybe you were refuge. Maybe she loved you. Those aren't mutually exclusive."

Silence pooled.

Finally Anton pushed the notebook over.

"Take it. Proof seldom lasts, but try."

Lucas tucked it into his backpack.

Coffee cooled between them.

Anton exhaled a long, dry laugh.

"She taught me one lesson: the closer you get, the more the world tilts. If you step right to the center, you slip off."

He met Lucas's stare.

"I'm alive because I stopped two steps shy."

"Yet you still search."

"I search carefully."

Barista poked her head through the curtain, signaled closing for midday break.

Anton stood.

He donned a wool coat frayed at cuffs.

At the exit he paused.

"If you keep chasing her, mark your memories. Tattoo them if you must. They'll fade faster than paper."

Lucas rose.

"I have to find her."

Anton's gaze filled with pity no anger could deflect.

"Then write your own name somewhere safe. Because if you get too close to her, you will disappear—*not her.*"

He left, doorbell jangling a funeral bell.

Lucas sat, pulse drumming between ribs.

Outside, rain cleared; sunlight speared puddles.

He paid, stepped into the street, breathed exhaust and pastry and wet stone.

He opened the notebook again.

One entry leapt: *KARLÍN — NOV 22 — S* Then an arrow to *VLTAVA — 23:45 — 55*

He recognized Karlín—the district housing Veselý's new company.

He pocketed the book.

His phone vibrated—text from Lenka: *Contact from detective. Veselý resurfaced under firm SOMA Security. Address attached.*

Lucas's skin prickled.

SOMA again.

He typed a reply: *On my way.*

On the tram he replayed Anton's warning.

Vanishing, not dying.

Identity peeled until even mirrors refused.

He tapped the reflection in the tram window; for now it answered.

He reached Karlín mid-afternoon.

Office block of tinted glass, lobby guarded by turnstiles.

A digital directory listed *SOMA SECURITY — Floor 5.*
Lucas memorized badge patterns, employee rhythms,
but knew he lacked credentials.
He retreated to a riverside bench, studying flow charts
in the notebook.
Times, trains, codes—perhaps escape routes.
At the margins Julia/Sophie/Karolina had doodled
circles swallowing squares, labeled *safe* and *false safe*.

He closed the book, palms sweating.
Anton's photographs resurfaced in his mind—each
moment of stolen joy.
He understood the lure: she offered warmth underneath
a ticking clock.

His own warmth sparked anew; love not dead, only
camouflaged.
He inhaled, counted: one, two, three, five, eight,
thirteen, twenty-one, thirty-four.
At thirty-four his pulse steadied.
He stood, hoodie damp from bench, and headed back
toward the hostel to plan, yet feeling the tilt Anton
warned about—streets bending like warped glass,
passersby blurring at edges.

Night approached on silent feet.
Lucas wrote his name and passport number in indelible
ink inside the notebook's cover.
Proof of self, in case.

After a restless meal he called Bauer in Berlin,
voicemail again.
Left a cryptic update: "Found a witness. Not delusional.

Please verify SOMA Security, Prague."
He stared at the send icon, wondering if the message would survive the trip.

He lined up Anton's photos, Julia's blurred stills, the market badge, the missing-person column, tracing a web.
At the center shimmered her mutable face.
He whispered: "I'm coming."

Then he remembered Anton's last look—resigned, almost fond.
Lucas opened the hostel wardrobe, searched for a surface unseen.
He carved his initials into the wooden backing with a pocket knife: **LS 06/25**.
A crude insurance policy, anchored in matter thicker than memory.

He lay on the bed, notebook clutched to chest, counting backwards this time, shredding the spiral down to one.
Outside, the city braced for another snowfall, erasing tracks before day could name them.

Lucas dreamed of Sophie fishing photographs from a river, each image washing clean until only water remained, and her soft voice repeating through it all: *stay two steps back, love—two steps back—or the current will take you whole.*

He woke just before dawn, name still etched in wood, self still intact, heart still determined.
For now, the world had not decided he was imaginary.

He dressed, tucked Anton's notebook close, and stepped into the corridor, ready to tilt with the day.

CHAPTER 7

EROSION

Rain peppered the hostel window like fingers drumming a warning.

Lucas hunched over the small desk, dawn light paling the room.

He powered up the laptop, fingers ready to comb Anton's notebook for clues.

The screen flicked to life, but the cursor moved before he touched the track-pad—sliding across icons, opening folders, selecting whole blocks of files.

For a heartbeat he thought he'd brushed the pad by accident.

Then the cursor jumped again, too quick, too deliberate, carving a rectangle around every document stamped with Julia's name.

He yanked his hands away.

The cursor kept hunting.

Right-click.

Delete.

Confirmation box appeared, vanished.

Another folder.

Delete.

Emails disappeared in flurries, subject lines blinking out like blown bulbs.

Lucas slammed the lid closed, severing the feed, pulse hammering.

He pulled the battery, shut the hostel Wi-Fi switch on the wall for good measure.

But in that ten-second gap, months of notes, screenshots, and photographs had slipped into digital ash.

He stared at the dark shell, breath shallow.
A cold, methodical voice in his head whispered: *They're wiping you.*

By noon his German phone lit with a company number—Berlin headquarters.
He took the call in the hostel stairwell, concrete echoing each syllable.

HR director Frau Neumann spoke first, clipped politeness.
"Lucas, we've flagged irregularities in several client repositories that bear your credentials."
Behind her words lurked weight: legal, disciplinary, the grinding gears of process.

He said he'd been on approved leave.
She replied that the audit showed timestamps from the previous night—mass edits to sensitive datasets.
Another tone layered in: disappointment bending toward mistrust.

"You'll receive an official letter," she said.
"Until we clarify this, your system access is

suspended."
Lucas tried to protest, but the call ended on a chalk-screech dial tone.

He pressed the phone to his chest.
The beating underneath felt slower, as if his heart considered resignation.
Then adrenaline punched it forward again.

He logged in to his online banking from the hostel lobby computer—old hardware, green-tinged screen.
The security page requested two-factor authentication, accepted it, and unfurled his recent charges.

A €3,200 payment to **Hotel Nebozízek**.
Fine dining, bar tabs, spa services, all dated the night his phone captured the graffiti on the locked gate.
The invoice bore a signature: **J. Schwarz — guest of record**.
And below, his own card digits listed as primary guarantee.

Lucas leaned back, plastic chair groaning.
His last transaction, he knew, had been a cheap kebab near the hostel.
Everything else was smoke.

He clicked deeper: an airline ticket in his name, Prague to Dubai, business class, tomorrow at dawn.
He had never logged into the airline site.
A second ticket in the adjacent seat: **Karolina Vondráková**.

The computer whirred, indifferent.
He felt the floor tilt, an elevator dropping too fast.

An email alert chimed—inbox still accessible though
HR locked the work drive.
Subject line: *RE: URGENT*, from Martin.
Lucas opened.

> Just got the weirdest voice message from "you."
> Sounds like your accent, but not *you*.
> Said you're fine, you're "off the grid with Julia,"
> you quit the job, starting "new life."
> Wants me to forward a resignation letter
> attached.
> Dude, you okay?

Lucas clicked the audio attachment.
Static, then his own cadence, but vowels slightly
metallic, as if run through a throat made of wires.

*Hey Martin, it's Lucas—listen, I'm out. Julia and I
decided to disappear for a while. Don't worry, but
delete our old files, yeah? Tell the guys at the office I'm
sorry.*

Silence followed, as final as a slammed coffin.

He played it again.
Every intonation was almost perfect, yet the soul was
missing—a ventriloquist's draft.
Deep-fake tech, voice-cloning: the thought struck cold.

He typed back: *Not me. Hold everything.*

A reply bounced instantly: *Delivery failed — address does not exist.* Martin's inbox, erased?

Lucas's fingers hovered above the keyboard.
One friend, severed.
One employer, doubting.
One bank account, poisoned.
The erasure advanced like fire through dry grass.

Outside, clouds bunched above Prague Castle, bruised purple.
Lucas needed fresh air, proof of something physical.
He left the hostel, laptop battery pocketed in case, and walked.

Every block brought a new vibration to his phone until the notifications clotted the screen.
LinkedIn: *Your profile photo removed for policy violation.*
Slack: *Your workspace access revoked.*
Facebook: *We couldn't confirm your identity; account disabled.*
A lifetime of log-ins dissolving as he watched.

He crossed Legion Bridge, the Vltava churn below.
Tourists gawked at swans; none noticed the man losing his outline.

Halfway across he stopped, gripped the railing, forced slow breaths.
Counting steadied him: one, two, three, five—

But the next number snagged, mind fogging.
He leaned over the river, asked the water for calm.

Phone vibrated again—unknown caller.
He answered, voice raw.
No greeting, just a low murmur:
"Mr. Schwarz, your reservation is confirmed for tonight.
Presidential suite. Champagne upon arrival."
He tried to speak, found his throat sealed.
The caller continued, "If you need anything else for Ms.
Schwarz, let us know."
He managed a whisper: "Cancel."
The voice chuckled—soft, almost kind.
"I'm afraid the transaction is non-refundable."
Click.

Lucas watched ripples riffle along the Vltava's brown
surface, wondered if identity could sink like a stone.

Evening rolled in with sleet.
Back at the hostel he plugged the battery into the
laptop, kept Wi-Fi off, booted in safe mode.
The drive showed blank patches where directories had
lived.
But deep in a recovery partition he found shadow
files—metadata scraped as the deletions executed.

He ran a low-level viewer: timestamps, IP addresses,
process names.
Unfamiliar IP, Czech telecom range, tagged *SOMA-
RemoteD*.

A ghost in his machine branded by the same word looping through Anton's notebook.

He copied the log to a USB.
No sooner saved than the cursor jolted again—another remote session punching through the disabled adapter somehow.
Bluetooth exploit?
Printed text on the screen:

Stop looking, Lucas. We are amending the record. Take the flight.

He killed power, shredded the battery connection wires with hostel scissors, rendering the shell inert.
Evidence still lived in the USB.
He slipped it into a sock for safekeeping.

Lights flickered in the corridor—old wiring or interference.
Door pounded; hostel manager shouted, Czech words tumbling.
Lucas opened.
Two Prague officers flanked the manager.
One spoke English rough but clear:
"Mr. Schwarz, you must come with us. Bank fraud investigation."
Lucas's pulse spiked.
"I'm the victim, not the thief."
The officer's face held bureaucratic patience.
"You can explain at the station."

Lucas asked to bring his bag; they allowed.
He tucked in the USB, the notebook, Anton's photos.
In the squad car he watched neon smear across wet glass, city lights bending like molten glass.

At the precinct, paper-white fluorescents carved shadows under his eyes.
An investigator cited charges: unauthorized transactions, identity fabrication, potential corporate sabotage.
Lucas handed over the USB, told the story at staccato speed—Julia, Karolina, deleted files, voice-cloned messages.

The investigator listened, expression draining from interest to wary concern.
At the word *erasure* his brow rose, as if noting textbook symptom.
He excused himself.
Minutes later a social-services clinician entered with a clipboard.
Gentle smile, practiced.
She offered tea.
Asked how long Lucas had been under stress.
Asked if he'd ever been diagnosed.

He felt the net tighten, threads silk-soft yet steel-strong.
Bureaucracy was the spider, weaving disbelief until movement ceased.

Lucas stood, palms flat on the table.
"I'm not sick. Someone is editing reality."
His own declaration sounded unhinged in the sterile

room.

The clinician gently gestured for him to sit.

Her eyes flitted to the door where an orderly waited.

Fight surged.

Lucas pivoted, bolted past the orderly, down a hall, through a fire exit alarm howling.

Night air slapped him awake.

He sprinted, lungs tearing, dodged across a tram track, horns blaring.

Behind, shouts in Czech; no gunfire, thank God.

He vanished down an alley too narrow for pursuit cars, climbed a rusted ladder to a rooftop.

Knees shook; he crouched behind a chimney stack, breath fogging.

From his pocket he pulled the ring, cold against sweat-warm skin.

He whispered, "Julia, please."

Street sounds softened.

In the hush he heard her voice—not memory, but present—somewhere close, saying his name.

He rose, craned over the roof edge.

Below, a courtyard stippled with puddles.

Empty.

Only wind.

He sagged, slid down to sit on tar-paper.

His phone buzzed despite Do-Not-Disturb.

Text from unknown: *Look up.*

He did.

Across the next roof, barely lit by a hotel billboard glow,

a figure stood—slim, hair whipping, coat too thin for December.
She lifted a hand, almost a wave, almost a warning.

Lucas lurched to his feet, heart detonating hope.
But the figure stepped back, into dark, swallowed by the gap between buildings.

He shouted, voice ricocheting off brick, then rushed, searching rooftop edges for a crossing.
None.
Only shadow.

Sirens keened closer; squad lights jittered on walls.
Lucas backed away into deeper dark, gripping the ring and the USB as if they were the last atoms of himself still untampered.

Somewhere below a tram bell chimed, counting off distance.
He inhaled, forced the sequence through clenched teeth: one, two, three, five, eight, thirteen, twenty-one, thirty-four.
Memory still obeyed.
For now.

Yet job, bank, friends, even the police records—every scaffold that propped his existence—had begun to shake loose like rot-riddled beams under sudden weight.

He pressed palms together, felt blood pulse.
You are Lucas Schwarz, he told himself.
Born Munich, thirty-three years ago.
The urban cacophony argued back.

He rose, gathered courage, and slipped into a stairwell leading down the far side of the block, every step a gamble on which parts of the world might still agree he was real when he hit the pavement.

The rooftop door sighed shut above him, locking with a decisive click.
Lucas pocketed the ring, squared his shoulders, and walked into the maze of streets, carrying the splintering remains of his identity like a candle cupped against a hurricane wind—knowing that once the flame went out, he would be the next file silently dragged to trash, last chance for undo already expired.

CHAPTER 8

THE MIRROR WOMAN

Night welded itself to morning in a seam of sleepless hours.
Lucas paced the borrowed flat—an attic sublet whose tenant asked no questions so long as the rent slid uncounted into a worn envelope.
Rain tapped the skylight like hesitant code.
He kept one lamp on, low, watching its pool of light shrink each time clouds thickened.

He rehearsed a script for the next confrontation:
My files were erased.
My voice was cloned.
I have proof—logs, photographs, the Fibonacci notebook.
He tried different cadences, but every line sounded fevered, a conspiracy hissed through clenched teeth.

At 6:17 a.m. a soft knock.
Three taps, evenly spaced.
He froze, heartbeat clocking double.
Another knock, same pattern.

He crossed the creaking floorboards, pressed eye to the peephole.
A woman stood in the narrow hallway, coat draped like

tailored armor, hair in a sleek bun.
She held a compact umbrella, pearl-gray, collapsed but beaded with recent rain.
Her posture read neither threat nor plea, only what one might call official grace.

Lucas's breath snagged.
It was Julia.
Yet not Julia: shoulders squared to an angle Julia avoided, chin lifted half a degree higher.
Eyes the same color, but colder, mineral.
As if someone sanded memory off the irises.

He unlocked the chain, opened the door two inches.
The hallway's stale light spilled between them.

"Julia," he whispered.

She tilted her head, lips pared into a fraction of a smile that never reachéd the eyes.
"Good morning. I'm looking for Lucas Schwarz."
Her German bore a lighter accent than before—Swiss inflection, crisp vowels.

He swallowed. "That's me."

She nodded, businesslike.
"I'm Lea Wagner."
She removed a wallet from her bag—soft leather.
Flipped it open.
Inside: identity card stamped **Bundesrepublik Deutschland**.
Name: **Lea Marie Wagner**.
Date of birth a day earlier than Julia's.
Hologram shimmer intact.

A second plastic encased a passport photo—airport-photo-booth sterile, the bun pulled tight, expression regulation-bland.

He stared.
Her fingers were steady as she held the ID for inspection—a gesture practiced, perhaps from airport lines.

Lucas's mouth tasted metal.
"What do you want?"

Her voice stayed sanded flat.
"To ask you to stop contacting me."

He blinked.
"I haven't—"
She slipped a phone from her coat, tapped open an email thread.
Dozens of messages from *Lucas.Schwarz@—*, subject lines pleading: **Please call**, **I need to see you**, **We are married**.
Attached were photographs: his own face, the ring, the peach-market shot.

He felt the floor tilt.
Those were never sent by him.

"I didn't write those," he managed.

She raised a brow, not arguing, but not convinced.
"It doesn't matter. It needs to stop."
She returned the phone to her pocket.

"Julia," he repeated, softer, a question trying not to sound like a prayer.

Her eyes cooled a further degree.
"I am not Julia. I am not Karolina. I am certainly not your wife."

He inhaled, tasting dust.
"We lived together. Berlin. You left your ring."

She gave the faintest exhale, a signal of polite disbelief.
"My ring is here."
She lifted her left hand—there on the fourth finger sat an identical band, but flawless, unmarred.
He studied the engraving inside—exactly positioned but impossible to read from distance.
He instinctively touched his pocket where the ring he carried sat like a shard of origin.

Lea continued, tone patient as a doctor instructing a child.
"You have been following me. You broke into my life with stories of marriage. Last week you tried to access my apartment in Kampa. The caretaker filed a report."

Lucas shook his head so hard his vision blurred.
"I have never been to Kampa. I was hunted through Prague looking for you."

She regarded his panic with observational calm.
"This fixation is harmful to you and dangerous to me."

From her bag she produced a slim stack of papers—copies.
The top sheet: a restraining order request, unsigned by a judge but stamped *RECEIVED.*
Beneath: rental agreement for **Haštalská 9, Prague 1**, tenant **Lea Wagner**, approved last month.

Next: employment contract with **SOMA Security**, communications analyst.
ID badges, tax numbers, all fresh ink.

Lucas stared at the SOMA logo—sleek sans-serif S encircling a lens icon.
He felt bile.
"This is fabricated."

She tucked the pages away.
"In fifteen minutes officers will arrive to validate my report. Please be prepared to answer calmly."

"Why?" His voice broke on the single word.

She studied him a beat longer, as if weighing whether truth mattered.
Finally: "Because I told them you threatened me yesterday."

His mouth opened, soundless.
"I never—"

She eased the door wider with a deliberate step forward.
Up close the air around her smelled of bergamot, yes, but beneath it a faint trace of the hotel-scented soap he once teased her about.
Memory punched him.

He whispered, "Julia, look at me."

For the first time her composure flickered—something behind the eyes, a glitch of recognition maybe, or pity.
Then shutters closed again.

"You should seek help," she said, voice level.
"Voluntarily. It will be easier."

Two sets of footfalls echoed up the stairwell—solid, syncopated.
Police.
Lea raised her umbrella tip in a small farewell.
She turned, descending.
At the landing she paused, looked back.
Her lips moved—he thought he saw *thirty-four* form in silent breath—then she continued down.

He felt his knees fail the moment she was out of sight.
He caught the doorframe, breath shaking.

Policemen stepped into view—one older with paperwork, one younger with a cautious stance.
Lucas stood, palms open.
The older officer spoke Czech, then switched to English.
"Mr. Schwarz, may we come in?"

He nodded.
Inside, they scanned the disorder—maps, printouts, the dead laptop husk.
The officer asked about threats, about emails.
Lucas described hacks, voice fakes, the erasure.
Words spilled jagged; grammar fractured.
He knew he sounded like a storm trapped in a bottle.

Younger officer's gaze drifted to the walls—strings of twine linking photos, Anton's notebook pages pinned like insects.

A red thread circled the SOMA logo.
Under it: **Erase/Replace** scrawled in hurried pen.

The older officer's pen scraped forms.
"Miss Wagner has filed for protective order. She asserts you harassed her under delusional belief of marriage."
Lucas shook his head until it hurt.
"She *is* my wife."
"Can you produce a certificate?"
"It was stolen."
"Any witnesses?"
"Everyone who knew her forgets."
Silence thickened.
The officer's eyes carried the weight of experience: he had heard this cadence before, in other apartments, other midnight calls.
Delusion dressed as devotion.

He asked Lucas to consider a voluntary evaluation at **Bohnice Psychiatric Hospital**.
"Only to clarify your mental state, Mr. Schwarz."
Voluntary carried an unspoken alternative: involuntary.

Lucas thought of Anton's fourteen days behind locked doors, drooling medication onto plastic pillows.
He heard Lea's parting words: *It will be easier.*
He looked at his wall—evidence fragile, context missing.
He looked at the officers—calm, armed, procedural.
He closed his eyes, counted: one, two, three, five, eight.
On thirteen his breath steadied enough to speak.

"I'll come. Voluntarily."

The younger officer relaxed minutely.
They allowed him to pack a small bag: toothbrush, change of clothes, the USB hidden inside a sock.
The notebook he tucked into waistband under his sweater.
They asked him to leave the laptop.
He complied—it was already a corpse.

As they escorted him out, tenants cracked doors, eyes glinting.
Gossip seeded.
He kept head high, repeating the sequence under breath to drown whispers.

Street outside glistened from earlier rain.
A patrol car idled.
Lea stood beside it, talking to the policewoman he hadn't seen upstairs.
Umbrella now open—pearl gray against the muted backdrop.
They both looked up as Lucas emerged.

He met Lea's gaze across the hood.
She did not flinch, did not soften.
But her fingers—white-knuckled on the umbrella handle—twitched twice, a tiny tremor.
Signal? Residual empathy?
He couldn't tell.

The older officer opened the back door of the car, gestured.
Lucas slid in.

Glass smelled of sanitizer and past arrests.
Engine rumbled.
Lea's profile receded as the car pulled away.
She became a silhouette beneath a gray arc, rain
beginning again, umbrella rising like a shield.

He watched her until the street bent out of sight.
Only then did he close his eyes.
Darkness filled with rotary-wing echoes: words
spinning, names switching, a life rewritten in real time.
He pressed knuckles to lips, felt the notebook's outline
against his spine—last proof pressing back.

Sirens silent, city noise dimmed by closed windows, the
patrol cruised across bridges toward the northern
district.
Officers spoke low Czech; he understood scraps—
temporary, *observation*, *24 hours unless extended.*

He opened his eyes to the blur of tram wires overhead,
twisting like scribbles that the sky kept trying to erase.

Thirty minutes later the car turned through iron gates.
A campus of 19th-century pavilions, lawns soaked,
bare trees listing.
Psychiatrická nemocnice Bohnice etched above an
archway.
Brickwork the color of dried blood.

Inside reception, fluorescent light sunk deep into
creases of the floor nurse's uniform.
Intake forms emerged—name, date, voluntary tick box.
He signed.
Pen scratched slow.

The box beneath *Next of kin* he left blank.
He wanted to write *Julia*—but which one?

They catalogued belongings: phone (battery removed), wallet, watch.
USB they missed; hidden in the elastic of his sock.
Notebook they missed too.
He felt its square pressure, talismanic.

An orderly guided him to Ward F—Observation.
White door thunked.
Inside: pale walls, bed bolted to floor, window glass wired.
A desk, a chair, a discreet camera.
He sat on the bed, mattress stiff.

A resident psychiatrist entered—Dr. Kovář, spectacles fogged from outside air.
She offered water, introduced herself.
Asked: "Why do you think you're here?"
Lucas considered the ceiling, the fluorescents humming in Fibonacci intervals: 1…1…2…3…5…
He told her about missing wife, shifting names, erased files, voice clones, SOMA.
She listened, hands folded, expression flat but not cruel.
When he finished, she asked, "Do these events feel real, or like a film you were placed in?"

He wanted to shout, to smash the calm.
Instead he said, "Both."

Dr. Kovář nodded, noted.
"You understand why this presentation concerns the

police."

He nodded.

She explained he would stay overnight for assessment; medication offered only if agitation rose.

He declined.

She left.

The door sealed.

Outside, footsteps receded.

Lights dimmed into evening mode—still bright enough to chase dreams away.

Lucas stretched on the bed, notebook against spine.

Rain whispered against barred glass.

He mouthed the sequence, slower, letting each number anchor him in the room.

He thought of Lea's fingers twitching.

Perhaps a code: two twitches—Fibonacci start.

Or conscience.

He pictured walking into her new apartment, seeing walls bare of him, smelling a life sanitized of old echoes.

He saw her counting after midnight when she believed cameras couldn't see.

He vowed to find the slip—the seam where Julia's grief leaked through Lea's armor.

But first he had to survive this place, keep mind clear, proof intact.

He tapped the notebook's cover once, twice, thrice— then five times—pledging silence.

In the corridor someone screamed wordlessly, a long tearing wail.

Orderlies murmured.

Then silence folded over everything like the gray umbrella outside, skins within skins protecting fragile fictions from the weather.

Lucas closed his eyes.

Memory played footage of a summer market, peaches glowing, Julia-Karolina-Lea smiling over sunglass rims.

He whispered to the ceiling: "I remember."

The lights continued their hum, steady, indifferent.

For now, remembrance was enough.

CHAPTER 9

THE QUIET WARD

Morning slipped through reinforced glass in a dull wedge, illuminating the white-tiled corridor like the inside of a fish tank.

Lucas sat on the cot, shoulders hunched, blanket folded with military precision at his feet.

A night orderly had taken his pulse at 06:00 and left without a word, but he could still taste the rubber of the blood-pressure cuff on his forearm.

At 07:30 the door opened.

Nurse Adéla ushered in a paper tray: porridge, one apple slice, a plastic cup holding two small capsules—pale blue this time, not white.

"Change in regimen," she said, voice flat as a hallway echo.

He looked at the pills.

No label.

No dosage sheet.

Just anonymous chemistry.

He asked what they were.

She only repeated, "Regimen."

When he didn't reach for them, she placed the cup on the windowsill and left.

Lock clicked.

He stared at the capsules until the apple slice browned at the edges.

Memory tugged: Julia counting pills by moonlight, discarding the ones she didn't trust.

He slid the capsules into the folded blanket, hid them inside the pillowcase seam.

The porridge he ate, spoon by mechanical spoon.

At 08:10 Dr. Kovář entered with a clipboard haloed by morning glare.

Her glasses carried a thin film of fog; she wiped them on her sleeve with clinical economy.

"No phone privileges today," she said before he asked. "Your family declined a visit."

He almost laughed—family? There was no one left to call, but hearing it stated so plainly stripped another layer from his identity.

She scanned his chart.

"How are the thoughts?"

"Orderly," he lied, smoothing his voice.

"Any more voices?"

"No voices."

"No visual alterations?"

"Just fluorescent lights and gray walls."

She made a note.

"Sleep?"

"Six hours."

"Nightmares?"

"Only bureaucracy."

She looked up.

"Tell me more about bureaucracy."

He composed a smile that held.

"Long lines. Stamps. Doors that close before you reach them."

Her eyes rested on him, searching for tremors.

He steadied his breathing so each exhale matched the tick of the overhead clock.

Finally she nodded once, not fully convinced, but satisfied for now.

"We've moved you to quetiapine," she said.

"Milder. Helps regulate circadian rhythm."

He wanted to ask why he needed any of it.

Instead he said, "Thank you."

The politeness tasted sour, but it was a necessary flavor.

She stood to leave, then paused at the doorframe.

"Remember, Mr. Schwarz, sometimes the enemy sits within our own perception. Beware projections."

He nodded as if enlightened.

When she was gone he breathed out hard, felt sweat on his upper lip.

Enemy within.

A convenient truism, and maybe sometimes true, but not this time.

He was sure.

Almost sure.

He spent the rest of the morning pacing the small rectangle between door and window, counting footsteps to match the Fibonacci rhythm: one, one, two, three, five, eight, thirteen, twenty-one, thirty-four.

On thirty-four he reached the radiator, touched metal

coolness, pivoted, began again.

With every circuit he rehearsed sane replies, clipped and plausible.

He would need them.

Early release required a glass-smooth surface; no ripples.

Just before lunch he remembered the other USB stick—the first one, the real backup, not the one hidden in his sock.

Months ago he had dumped photo archives and draft chapters onto a thumb drive shaped like a silver key.

He kept it taped under the false bottom of Julia's jewellery box back in Berlin.

But that box sat on his dresser in the apartment that now felt as distant as a childhood town.

Unless…

Unless he had carried the key-drive in his laptop bag during the Prague trip.

An echo of memory flickered: sliding a key-shaped stick into an inner pocket with his passport, thinking *redundancy never hurts.*

Had he removed it when the police grabbed his belongings?

He couldn't remember.

He rummaged through the small duffel that the guards hadn't bothered to inspect deeply—two shirts, one paperback, the hijacked USB, toothbrush still in wrapper.

No silver-key drive.

Heart sank.

He emptied every seam.
Still no.

He clenched the bag, searching deeper in memory:
packing at the hostel; the key-drive slipping into his
jacket.
But the jacket was now at the police property room.

He sat on the bed, adrenaline nudging clarity.
If he could convince Kovář of stability, he might collect
his possessions on discharge.
The drive might still be there, unnoticed, holding
images before the erasure waves washed them blank.

Afternoon group therapy followed lunch—lukewarm
soup, stale bread, one-hour circle chaired by a burly
psychologist with kind eyes.
Lucas joined nine others on plastic chairs.
He listened more than spoke, nodding with empathy
whenever someone described the hum of invisible
insects or a mother's voice emanating from light
fixtures.
When his turn came, he said, "I'm here because stress
blurred lines between work and life.
Sometimes I chased patterns that weren't patterns."
He folded hands in his lap, elbows relaxed, gaze
steady.
The psychologist offered mild praise for insight.
Lucas thanked him.

After group a nurse led him to the courtyard—a ten-
minute courtyard break, chain-link fence, winter weeds.
Sky pewter gray, birds absent.

Couple patients shuffled smokes; one muttered Czech curses at clouds.

Lucas paced gravel, inhaling cold air that stung lungs awake.

A camera watched from above; he kept expression neutral.

Inside the windbreak of his coat he counted, let the numbers thrum like a secret motor.

That evening he forced down dinner, swallowed the new pills under nurse supervision but held them behind molars, later spitting into toilet tissue flushed away.

He kept a mental ledger: two capsules hidden in pillow, two more gone to sewer.

No sedation clouded his senses.

He needed mind sharp.

The next morning, more evaluation.

Dr. Kovář asked him to draw a clock at 10:15, recite months backward, identify emotions in pictured faces.

He complied calmly, drawing hands with purposeful strokes, recounting months as if listing ingredients, naming each emotion with a subdued empathy.

She took notes, eyes narrowing when she couldn't find an edge.

"Where do you see yourself after discharge?" she asked at last.

"Back at the office," he lied.

"I've overlooked boundaries. I'll rebuild trust."

He waited for skepticism.

It came, faint, but she only said, "Insight is progress."

She scheduled a family meeting, though none would come; hospital policy.

He suggested a video call with his mother; he knew the number she kept for emergencies.

Kovář approved, but technical staff reported line failure—convenient.

He pretended mild disappointment, nothing more.

That afternoon an orderly escorted him to the small gym as test of responsibility.

He jogged the treadmill, gentle pace, let sweat sheet his skin but not his mind.

Kept breathing even.

The orderly noted compliance in a chart.

Points accrued toward early review.

Back in the room, he unfolded Anton's notebook when no one watched, studying train codes and SOMA links. One diagonal line pointed from Prague to Berlin with an annotation: *dl* followed by a date three weeks ahead. *Download? Deadline?*

He closed the book as keys rattled in the door.

Two days blurred into routine: pills hidden and flushed, therapy attended, bedding folded, questions answered with measured calm.

The internal storm stayed masked.

On the evening of the third day, Nurse Adéla whispered, "Doctor considering step-down status."

Lucas thanked her, kept expression modest.

Inside, his pulse hammered triumph.

Friday morning, board review.
A long table of clinicians, cups of bitter coffee, overhead projector flickering patient metrics.
Dr. Kovář summarized: initial presentation acute, orientation stable, insight fair, risk moderate, compliance good.
She recommended conditional discharge: daily outpatient visit, medication adherence, family support.
Others murmured assent.
One junior psychiatrist argued he showed "structured delusional system centering on partner identity."
Kovář lifted a brow.
"He distinguishes internal experience from shared reality now.
Progress notable."
Vote taken.
Discharge approved.

Lucas exhaled, tension leaking from shoulders.
Paperwork queued.
He signed release forms, accepted a starter pack of the blue capsules—quetiapine label printed this time.
He pocketed them, planning an accident in the nearest trash.

Property room next.
A young clerk in headphones handed over sealed belongings: laptop shell, jacket, wallet, phone minus SIM, a tangled charger.
Lucas signed and scanned items, heart drumming when finger brushed the jacket's inner pocket.

A firm rectangular bulge pressed the lining.
He kept relief off his face.

Outside the gates, late afternoon light hung pale gold.
Cold air smelled of coal smoke and pine.
He walked two tram stops before ducking into a public
WC, locked a stall, pulled out the silver key-drive.
Polished metal gleamed.
He exhaled a broken laugh.

He slotted it into the dead laptop; the machine still
booted from battery though screen cracked.
Explorer opened: a single folder, */Julia_Backup*.
Inside: hundreds of files—JPEGs, PDFs, email
exports—most dated weeks before the electronic
erasures.
He clicked one at random: a selfie of them on the
couch, both clear, both smiling, timestamp intact.
He clicked another: their marriage certificate scan,
signatures legible.
Proof.

He copied the entire folder onto the still-hidden USB for
redundancy, then onto the laptop's intact SD card slot.
Multiple seeds in case one burned.

He closed the lid, heart racing with possibility, and
flushed the blue pill bottle down the WC.
Quetiapine rattled in plastic as it swirled away.

In the mirror above the sink he saw stubble, eyes
rimmed red, yet the reflection was solid, unblurred.
He touched the glass.
It felt cool, definite.

Outside, snow began to fall—thin flakes swirling sideways in the wind.

He headed south toward the river, each step synced with numbers he whispered through steam-white breath.

One.

One.

Two.

Three.

Five.

Eight.

Thirteen.

Twenty-one.

Thirty-four.

On thirty-four he straightened spine, lifted chin.

He still had to decode Anton's final note, track Veselý, confront SOMA.

But he carried evidence now, tangible and redundant. Identity was a door, and he held its keys.

At the tram stop he scanned faces.

No Lea.

No police.

Just commuters shaking snow from shoulders.

He boarded, sat by the window, watched the city drift by—a city that had tried to sand him away.

He tapped the pocket where the key-drive rested, a heartbeat under metal.

His phone buzzed—new SIM, new number he'd bought at a kiosk.

A single SMS arrived from an unknown Czech line:

Sometimes the enemy is within ourselves. Sometimes it's standing right behind us.

He twisted in the seat—no one suspicious, only a kid scrolling music, a woman knitting.
He tucked the phone away, smile thin.

The tram rattled toward Centrum, tracks sparking under fresh snow.
Lucas closed his eyes, let the wheels drum the sequence for him, faster and faster, spiraling toward whatever waited in the hub of this widening pattern— ready at last to meet it on ground that numbers, files, and memory could prove was real.

CHAPTER 10

FOLDERS OF SMOKE

The snow kept falling, lazy and silent, as Lucas rode the tram back toward the attic flat.

He gripped the silver key-drive in his fist, thumb worrying the teeth that gave it its "key" shape.

Evidence hummed there, wanting eyes.

He forced himself to wait until he reached the attic, door bolted, lamp lit, kettle hissing.

The laptop booted with its spider-web crack across the upper corner.

He slid the drive home.

Directory opened: **/Archive/Full_Backup_J**.

Two sub-folders: **Photos_Raw** and **Logs**.

He clicked **Photos_Raw**.

Thumbnails tiled the screen like postage stamps from countries he'd never visited—Paris, Lisbon, Oslo, Dubrovnik, Tel Aviv.

In every frame Julia stood beside a different man, posture intimate yet composed.

Her hair length changed, color shifted, eyes hidden behind sunglasses, but the small mole at the base of her neck never moved.

Lucas clicked one at random.

Murano, Italy—she leaned over a canal rail, arm looped through a man's elbow.

Exif data: *Shot 12-09-2016, Nikon D5300.*

Photographer credited: *anton.weiss*

Lucas's stomach flipped—Anton never mentioned Italy.

Next file: Cappadocia, sunrise balloons.

Photographer name *seb.kruty*.

Date stamp *03-05-2018*.

Man's smile bright, arm around her waist, balloon basket between them.

A footnote in Anton's notebook had once muttered about a Czech teacher named Sebastian Krutý who "vanished after Cappadocia trip."

Lucas opened dozen more:—Julia dyed platinum, Berlin street art tour, companion a French cartoonist.— Julia blond pixie cut, standing in Reykjavík snow beside a Danish banker.

In each, she faced the lens, the man turned slightly toward her, as if the photographer mattered less than her approval.

He zoomed into every image.

No blur.

No erasure.

The ghosts only existed in Lucas's life; here she allowed herself to be permanent.

Halfway through the set, one photo clawed his breath away.

Prague, winter night, sodium lights painting brick

amber.

Julia—hair dark, chin-length, unmistakable—stood arm in arm with a serious-faced man wearing hospital scrubs.

They posed before the entrance of **Nemocnice Na Františku**, the small hospital along the Vltava.

Exif tag *shot by maria.leitner.*

Date *14-02-2019*—Valentine's Day.

Caption in the IPTC notes: *Jakub safe now.*

Lucas leaned back, ribs tight.

Jakub Havel—the name Anton's detective report had listed as "missing radiology tech," last seen leaving that same hospital.

Police concluded he "emigrated for work," case closed.

Here he smiled next to Julia, alive, two months before his vanishing.

Lucas saved a copy to the laptop's desktop, eyes glazing with dread.

One pattern emerged from the mosaic: she encircled men, left when their lives began to bend, their records to blur.

He pictured a serpent shedding skins, leaving each identity curling empty in the archives she never truly meant to hide.

He clicked **Logs**.

Dozens of CSV files—dates, GPS strings, MAC addresses.

One labeled **google_location_history.json**.

He opened it in a viewer.

Millions of latitude-longitude pairs scrolled, each entry

tagged *device_id: pixel2_julia*.
He filtered for the months they'd shared an apartment in Berlin.

Every evening from 18 July to 28 November 2024, the phone pinged one of three clusters: a coworking space in Mitte, a riverfront hostel, and a Kreuzberg studio address unfamiliar to Lucas.

Not once did the coordinates settle on their Friedrichshain flat.

Julia slept elsewhere, commuted to Lucas like an actor arriving for her scene.

He loaded Berlin municipal records.
Apartment registry listed only "Lucas Schwarz, single."
Lease co-signature line blank, untouched.
He felt air thinning, as if knowledge burned oxygen.

Next log entry: **bluetooth_pairings.txt**.
Device IDs matched his laptop, his phone—but timestamps pre-dated the day they first met.
She'd synchronized to him before he existed in her world, before chance introduced them on Petřín Hill.
Chance had been engineered.

Lucas stood, paced the creaking boards, brain filing shock behind fury.
He spoke aloud to the room, to the boiled-dry kettle, to the dust motes:
"Deliberate. Years. We were a project."
His voice sounded flat, as though the sentence bounced off a vacuum.

He opened another log: **expenses.csv**.

Flights booked in his name—sometimes with stolen numbers, sometimes processed and refunded before statement cycles.

She'd learned to debit his accounts just long enough to leave breadcrumbs, then reverse charges so the bank missed them, but not forensics.

There were Ferris-wheel rides in Lyon, tango lessons in Buenos Aires—cities Lucas had never breathed yet had "paid" to visit.

The last folder: **Draft_Emails**.

Dozens of text files containing email templates in his voice—breakup letters, resignations, apologies, confessions—never sent, but ready to launch.

He opened one titled **LUCAS_RESIGN_FULL.txt**—the same language that had spooked Martin.

She'd stored versions for each employer, each language.

Scalpel-fine mimicry.

He swiped a trembling hand over his face.

The timeline now met the horizon: Julia, Karolina, Sophie, Lea—identities unrolled like train stations; men boarded, disembarked, vanished into side tunnels.

Lucas saw how she mapped each life, inserted herself exactly where need intersected vulnerability, curated affection, then folded reality around her like origami until outsiders doubted the paper's original shape.

When threat loomed—police, jealousy, suspicion—she triggered the erasure sequence: corrupt photos, spoof charges, psychiatric flags, remote deletions.

113

SOMA, her employer, provided the tools.
Maybe she *was* SOMA.

He stared at the cracked screen, a subtle tremor in his neck.
Dr. Kovář's warning re-echoed: *enemy within ourselves.*
What if that "within" was not madness but infiltration, a Trojan woman coded to look like love?

Lucas selected the whole backup folder, compressed it, encrypted the archive with a passphrase he had never shared.
He uploaded the file to a new Proton Drive account created just now, two-factor via a new SIM.
He shared it with his own secondary address, with Anton, with journalist Petra Černá, with Lenka Vondráková—anyone whose memory still stubbornly held Julia's outline.
Redundancy, like cairns across shifting dunes.

When the transfer bar hit 100 %, he ejected the drive, slipped it into his wallet behind a faded student ID.
Proof would travel with him until he could place it in hands immune to deletion.

He sat again, breathing through the aftershocks.
One thought surfaced, calm as black ice: *Confront her, and she'll launch the final protocol.*
But what was the final protocol?
Total erasure?
A deep-fake confession leading to prison?

An "accidental" disappearance where his own GPS trail stopped at a bridge rail?

He opened Anton's notebook, flipped to the diagonal Berlin-Prague arrow.
Date three weeks ahead.
An overlay plan?
Maybe her cycle always ended with a hospital photo—caregiver, witness, scapegoat—then a second arrow out.
Jakub's hospital shot marked his final weeks; Anton had one at Vienna's Klinik Ottakring; Lucas's might be scheduled already.

He scanned **Photos_Raw** again, sorting by filename. Every set ended with a picture outside a medical facility:—Florence, 2015, Santa Maria Nuova, Julia beside accountant Marco Galilei (missing 2016).—Zürich, 2017, University Hospital, Julia with lawyer Nadim Heiss (missing 2018).
Pattern undeniable.
Hospitals were portals—places to gather ID data, maybe medical records for forging prescriptions, maybe to frame "patient histories" for later psychiatric claims.

A chill walked up his spine.
His own file at Bohnice already contained notes on delusion.
She'd begun drafting his erasure years before they met.
He whispered, "You were never improvising."

Snow thickened outside the skylight, world paling to gray.

Lucas rubbed his eyes, exhaustion layering like sediment.

But action mattered now, not awe.

He packed the laptop, notebook, passport, backup drive, burner phone.

Left kettle unplugged, lamp off.

He locked the attic door and taped a note on the inside:
L + J, I remember.

If she returned, he wanted her to see resistance first.

Down the stairwell he counted steps—one, one, two, three, five…

By thirty-four he reached the street, breath steady.

Tram wires sagged under snow.

He headed toward Karlín and the SOMA office block— source of remote deletions, digital ghosts.

He would not storm in yet; observation first, like she taught him.

Halfway there his phone buzzed.

New message from an unknown Proton address:

Some mirrors are built to shatter what looks into them. Turn back, Lucas.—L

He typed nothing in reply.

Instead he lifted the camera he'd brought—Anton's old DSLR—and photographed the message screen, the snow, the street number behind him.

More proofs in case mirrors broke.

At SOMA's glass façade he stood across the tramway, watching night staff swipe badges.
He spotted a silhouette at a fifth-floor window—slim, bun pinned tight, shoulders squared.
Lea.
She stared down at the street as if expecting him.
He stepped deeper into the alcove of a closed bistro, out of her sight, but kept eyes on the reflection in the door glass.
Her outline remained, backlit by blue monitor glow.

Lucas knew he would eventually enter that building.
But not yet.
First, he would deliver the archive to Petra Černá, whose newsroom valued old-school paper trails, then to Lenka, whose grief sharpened into righteous blade.
Allies anchored memory.
He turned away, snow squealing under boots.

Behind, the window light disappeared; Lea's shift over, or plan adapting.
Lucas did not look back.
He walked south toward the river, each breath blooming white, each step pressing numbers into drifts.
Evidence vivid in his pocket, shadows vivid at his heels, he felt the deception's timeline snap taut like a garrote—and for the first time imagined it breaking in his hands instead of around his throat.

The snow kept falling, covering tracks yes, but also preserving them—stenciling every footfall in cold relief until daylight or danger burned them away.
Lucas quickened pace, determined to leave enough

prints, enough files, enough witnesses that this time, when she slit reality to slip through, the world would notice the seam and pull her back, frame by frame, photo by photo, until the truth stood in full resolution and could not be deleted.

CHAPTER 11

PAPER TRAILS

Lucas stood in the shadow of a sycamore, collar up, breath clouding in the frosted evening.

Across the street, Lea—now passing as **Dr. Lara Novaková**—let herself into a fifth-floor flat in a renovated Art Deco block.

New name on the door buzzer, new haircut cropped high, same deliberate grace.

She carried only a slim leather laptop bag and the pearl-gray umbrella.

Lucas trained Anton's old DSLR on the entrance.

Click: Lea turning the key.

Click: the landlord passing her a welcome folder.

Click: the hallway light dying behind her.

He checked the timestamp on each frame, then slipped the camera back under his coat.

He kept watch for an hour.

No visitors, no deliveries.

When lights inside finally blinked off room by room, he withdrew, boots whispering on snow.

A tram bell chimed far off—the city's slow metronome.

—

He met **Petra Černá** in Café Slavia the next morning. She arrived with wind-whipped hair, recorder already rolling.

Petra sniffed skepticism but wore curiosity like cologne. A veteran of unsolved pages: child vanishings, union-bank frauds, a cult outside Brno that worshiped shortwave static.

She ordered black tea, no sugar.
Lucas laid the flash drive on the marble tabletop.
"Backups," he said.
"Metadata. Exif. Logs. Six men. One woman."
Petra arched a brow.
"I thought there were dozens."
"Six with a full pattern."

He gave her names, dates, last-known sightings, hospital photos:

- **Marco Galilei** — Florence accountant, missing 2016.
- **Nadim Heiss** — Zürich lawyer, missing 2018.
- **Jakub Havel** — Prague radiology tech, missing 2019.
- **Anton Weiss** — survived Vienna, psychiatric hold 2021.
- **Sebastian Krutý** — Czech teacher, disappeared after Cappadocia 2018.
- **Lucas Schwarz** — sitting opposite her, on borrowed time.

Petra listened, fingers steepled.

 "You realize how this sounds—one femme fatale conjuring ghost files across Europe?"

"Not femme fatale," Lucas said.

"Programmer. Social engineer."

He told her of doctored bank charges, voice-cloned messages, the medical notes at Bohnice, the restraining order that wasn't.

She played with a spoon, eyes narrowing as facts stacked.

"Evidence, not theory," she repeated.

"I print nothing without hard proof."

Lucas slid across three photos: Lea unlocking her new flat; the hospital shot with Jakub; the Google-location JSON printed, coordinates highlighted.

"Hard enough?"

"Harder," she said.

"Files can be faked. I need chain of custody."

He produced the camera, scrolled through raw images, Exif intact, GPS tags matching his phone's.

Petra's lips twitched—the first sign of interest cracking doubt.

"What does she want?" Petra asked.

Lucas shook his head.

"Maybe leverage. Maybe research. Maybe she courts men who carry certain access—finance, legal, medical, data."

He tapped the list: accountant, lawyer, hospital tech, teacher with university IT login, novelist with corporate clients.

"Data," Petra echoed.

"Medical, financial, personal."

She considered, then opened her tablet, pulling police bulletins.

Nadim's case file redacted; Marco's closed; Jakub's tidy footnote.

She frowned: reports sanitized.

"This many coincidences corrupt the odds."

Lucas unrolled Anton's notebook, pointing at an arrow from Prague to Berlin with tomorrow's date.

"Could be her exfil window."

Petra leaned closer.

Scribble read *Frant-Hauptbahnhof 05:10*.

"Night train," she murmured.

"And you'll follow?"

Lucas nodded.

Petra tapped recorder off.

"One condition," she said.

"You share every byte in real time. Geolocation, ticket stubs, CCTV grabs. No romantic heroism."

"I need public exposure," Lucas said.

"She erases quietly. A spotlight muzzles her."

Petra's smile flickered.

"Sunlight is antiseptic."

Deal struck, they drafted a plan:—Petra would request the hospital's entry logs under press transparency.— Lucas would stake Lea's building, capture travel preparations.—Together they'd corroborate the six men, map IP trails to SOMA servers.

Petra slid the flash drive into her satchel.
"Chain of custody begins now."

—

That night Lucas camped in a café opposite Lea's building, earphones feeding police-band static.
At 22:14 Lea emerged, a roll-aboard suitcase matching her coat.
Lucas snapped photos, paid the bill, tailed at half a block.

She walked direct to Masarykovo station, scanned a QR code at a kiosk—ticket printed: **Prague → Berlin**, departure 05:10 via night car.
Lucas photographed the screen, texted Petra: *She's booking.*
Petra replied with a link: a leaked SOMA pitch deck claiming "identity resiliency solutions" for private clients.
Bottom line: they specialized in sanitizing digital footprints.
Lucas felt vindication flare.

—

Pre-dawn cold rattled the train platform.
Lucas kept three cars behind, hood low.
Petra, remote but awake, coached via encrypted chat:
Stay visible to station cameras. If you vanish, we shout.

Lea boarded Sleeper Car 7, compartment 12.
Lucas found an empty seat in an adjoining coach.

The train lurched out, city lights surrendering to rural dark.

He dozed lightly, waking each time the train braked.
At 06:40 border agents walked aisle-to-aisle.
Lucas handed passport—no flags, thanks to early morning bureaucracy.
Agent moved on.

He crept toward Car 7.
Corridor deserted, curtains drawn.
Compartment 12 door closed, light under gap.
He lifted Anton's camera, adjusted ISO high, flipped mirror, and slotted the lens to the peephole crack.
Click.
Inside, Lea sat at the fold-down desk humming.
Laptop open, phone wired.
She uploaded files, progress bar blue.
Click.
He zoomed: folder name *exfil_DL*.

Data exfiltration in motion.
Lucas texted Petra the images.
She responded: *Getting server traces now.*

A conductor approached.
Lucas stashed camera, shuffled toward toilet, heartbeat thudding.
Through the window he glimpsed first rays of dawn routing lavender along cloud bellies.
New day.
Another skin for her.

—

Berlin Hauptbahnhof at 10:27—steel arches, hiss of brakes, rush-hour chaos.

Lucas exited the opposite side of the platform, phone streaming location to Petra.

Lea wheeled her suitcase toward the taxi rank.

Lucas hired the next cab, signaled driver to tail at distance.

Twenty minutes later they stopped at a boutique hotel in Prenzlauer Berg.

Lea paid, disappeared inside.

Lucas snapped facade, license plate, timestamp. Sent all to Petra.

Working city permits, she replied.
Police still cagey, but Heiss family cooperating.

—

Petra's newsroom occupied an old printworks; ink ghosts haunted corners.

Lucas joined her in a glass pod stacked with dossiers.

Whiteboard at his back now bore six headshots and arrows:

GALILEI → N

HEISS → CH

HAVEL → CZ

WEISS → AT

KRUTÝ → TR

SCHWARZ → DE

Petra pointed at connecting dots: timeframe overlap, similar hospital appearances, phone pairing logs. She'd cross-checked airline manifests and found Lea sharing flights with Jakub weeks before he vanished. Hospital security footage missing for all nights she visited.

"We print this," she said, "we need final forensic confirmation: her passport data, her employer contract, SOMA statements."
Lucas produced the camera's SD card: Lea's latest alias, the exfil upload.
Petra smiled, thin and sharp.
"Enough for a teaser."

She drafted copy: *"Serial Identity Artist Linked to European Disappearances—Exclusive."*
Graphics team overlaid a timeline.
Legal reviewed, demanded disclaimers until evidence reached court standard.

Petra leaned across the table.
"If we publish tonight, she'll bolt underground. We risk losing her."
Lucas shook his head.
"Spotlight freezes her long enough for warrants."

Petra chewed a fingernail—rare crack in composure.
"Police cooperation is thin. If she's got officials on payroll…"
Lucas placed a palm flat.
"She's writing my disappearance. I need public ledger first."

Petra inhaled, weighing ethics against stakes.

Finally: "Six p.m. We drop a teaser. Full investigation Sunday morning. Twenty-four hours to harvest reaction."

Lucas nodded.

She stood, grabbed her coat.

"I'll press city court for a gag motion in case SOMA threatens. You keep eyes on her."

As Lucas turned to leave, Petra caught his elbow.

"Lucas—proof, not theory. If any element fractures, we lose everything."

He patted the camera.

"I'll bring concrete."

—

Night fell blue-black.

Lucas camped in a bakery across from Lea's hotel.

6:03 p.m. — his phone lit with Petra's headline: **THE SHAPE-SHIFTER NEXT DOOR**.

Banner photo: Julia's hospital pose with Jakub, faces sharpened.

Sub-header: *Six men erased, corporate firm implicated.*

Within minutes social feeds exploded: hashtags *#GhostFiancée*, *#SOMAcoverup*.

Lucas refreshed comment threads.

A new account posted: *fake news. filed defamation.*

The user icon was SOMA's lens.

Inside the lobby Lea emerged, phone to ear, expression icy.

Lucas filmed through the window as she argued with

someone unseen, hand slicing air.

Taxicabs lined; she ignored them, choosing instead an unmarked black sedan that rolled up moments later.

He photographed plate, texted Petra.

Running plate.

Her reply seconds fast.

Registered to corporate fleet under shell firm.

Lucas hurried out, hailed a motor-bike courier with seat to spare.

"Follow that sedan," he said, cliché so thick it startled the rider into a grin.

They tailed across Mitte, past Parliament, toward outskirts.

Snow dusted asphalt; rider kept distance.

At a closed industrial park the sedan slipped through a security gate.

Lucas paid the driver, vaulted a side fence, camera bouncing against ribs.

Warehouse number 11 glowed dim.

Inside, rows of servers thrummed—a field of LED stars.

He crouched behind crates, lens zoomed.

Lea paced beside a technician, pointing to monitors.

Data streams scrolled code like green rain.

He captured every frame.

A guard coughed behind him.

Lucas ducked, heart slamming.

Footsteps receded—lucky blind spot.

He slipped back out, adrenaline spiking into nausea.

—

Back at Petra's office near midnight, he dumped new footage onto her workstation.
She scrubbed frames, eyes Wide.
"This is their purge site," she whispered.
"Live deletion."

She rang Jakub Havel's brother via Signal, confirmed that archive emails vanished tonight.
Pattern held: story goes live, they nuke residuals.
Petra exhaled, leaned over keyboard.
"We have the smoking server."

She phoned her editor, pitched a second-wave piece:
Inside the Erasure Factory.
Editor cursed joyfully, green-lit.

But legal still needed official logs.
Petra's phone dinged: city utility pass-codes from a source; access to warehouse power bills.
Enough to link SOMA to shell company.
"Tomorrow dawn we'll raid with cameras."

She turned to Lucas.
"Go rest. We'll storm the fortress together."
Lucas shook his head.
"Rest later."

He stepped to the window, city shimmering under snow.
Below, a silver hatchback idled too long, lights off.
He photographed it, reflex now automatic.
The back-seat shape glowed phone screen blue, driver unseen.
SOMA watchers.

He pivoted to Petra.
In her eye glinted the same mix of fear and thrill.
"We opened the door," she said.
"Now we keep it open."

Lucas felt the weight of six men behind him—two lost,
one dead, three breathing but bruised.
He squeezed the camera body until knuckles blanched.
"This time she doesn't step through without light."

He lifted the lens again, aimed at the dark city where
Lea might already be rewriting beams, and clicked—
shutter crisp, evidence born, theory buried under grain,
picture after picture after picture until dawn.

CHAPTER 12

COLD FRAMES

He found her on a Tuesday morning when the city still yawned itself awake.

Kaffeehaus Adler, vaulted ceilings, brass lamps, the hiss of an espresso line that never slept.

Lucas took a table in the back, coat on, camera in the courier bag at his feet.

The barista asked for his order; he asked for nothing, only water.

Hands shook; he jammed them beneath the table and waited.

Lea stepped in at 08:17, precisely as Petra's source had predicted.

Hair newly chestnut, bob smoothed curtly against jawline.

Tailored black trousers, ivory blouse, camel coat slung over one arm.

She carried a navy leather folio, barely thicker than a tablet.

Lucas's pulse sprinted.

He stood before he realized it.

Glassware tinkled.

Lea saw him, paused one breath, then approached—

no surprise, no retreat.
Just the tempo of a well-timed waltz.

"Lucas."
Cold greeting, no question mark.

"Lea," he said, forcing the name through teeth.
Then softer: "Julia."

She slid the folio onto his table, sat opposite, legs crossing with effortless grace.
"You should truly stop calling me that," she said.
"Wrong name. Delusion is a prison you built."
Voice calm, unhurried, texture of velvet chilled in dry ice.

Lucas studied her face, searchlight eyes scanning for any crack.
Mole at base of neck glinted beneath collar—unchanged, yet she carried it like a forgery.

He leaned forward.
"You started wiping the servers last night. Petra has the footage."

Lea smoothed a stray hair behind ear, one elegant motion.
"Petra's article was libelous fiction. It's gone now. Laws of entropy."
She opened the folio.
Inside, a neat stack of documents:—German passport in the name **Dr. Lara Nováková**.—Czech resident permit.—Medical license from Charles University.
Each embossed, holographic, watermark crisp like fresh winter air.

She placed them before him one by one, sliding as though across an operating tray.

"Scan the chip, call the embassy, test them under UV. They will bleed authenticity."

She waited.

Lucas didn't touch them; the edges seared his gaze.

"Identity," she said, "is a covenant with systems. You broke yours."

He tasted copper, fought the tremor in his voice.

"Jakub Havel. Nadim Heiss. Marco Galilei. Sebastian Krutý. Anton."

He left his own name last.

"They trusted you."

No flinch.

She just breathed a small, theatrical sigh.

"Men with holes seek women who promise wholeness. I never promised permanence."

Lucas's chair scraped when he jerked closer.

"Where are they?"

"Marco enjoys life in São Tomé. Nadim volunteers in Oman. Jakub married an engineer in Cyprus. People reinvent."

"You killed one."

"The Swiss accident? A misstep on a cliff is gravity's fault."

Her equanimity was an ice sheet—dangerous to stand upon, impossible to break bare-handed.

A patrol car whooped outside.
Lucas felt it vibrate glass in the window panes.
Lea's lips curved a millimeter.

"You're sick, Lucas," she said gently, as if diagnosing a mild fever.
"Dangerous. You threaten me, my employer, random bystanders. You attacked me at the warehouse yesterday."

"I never touched you."
He realized too late that shouting bled desperation.
Heads turned.
Barista's eyebrows climbed.

Lea gathered her papers neatly.
"I warned you to seek help voluntarily. Now you'll do so under mandate."

The café door swung.
Two uniformed officers entered, scanning.
Lea lifted a hand—fingernails nude, civilized.
They approached.

Officer Müller spoke first, German tinged with East-Berlin burr.
"Lucas Schwarz?"
Lucas nodded, throat tight.

"You are detained on charges of stalking, harassment, and issuing threats of violence."
"Proof?" Lucas rasped.

The second officer produced a printed dossier—
screenshots of emails, voice transcripts, even a

doctored video of Lucas outside the warehouse yelling "I will ruin you."
Deep-fake stitching still visible at edges, but close enough for bureaucracy.

Lea rose, collected her coat, looked down with curated pity.
"I truly hope you heal."
She turned, heels ticking tile, left through the revolving door.

Lucas's world narrowed to cuffs cold on wrists, a wallet bagged, camera confiscated.
Patrons stared, half-curious, half-terrified.
The barista whispered, "Gute Besserung," a waiter's reflexive wish for recovery.

—

Police station hallways smelled of Lysol and tired coffee.
Lucas sat in Interview Room B—white, windowless, hum of CCTV overhead.
A sergeant leafed through a file, brow furrowed.
"Mr. Schwarz," he said, "your name is flagged."
He pointed to a red banner across the record: **MENTAL HEALTH ALERT — APPROACH CAUTIOUSLY.**

Lucas swallowed a laugh that would shake him apart.
"I'm not violent," he whispered.
"I'm evidence."

Sergeant continued, almost kind.
"Psychiatric evaluation recommended before bail."
He slid a single sheet forward—Bohnice discharge note

amended overnight: **Patient exhibits relapse, fixated on fictitious spouse.**
Signature looked like Dr. Kovář's but the date typed hours earlier.

Lucas pressed fingertips to the table, grounding.
"Check Kovář's phone. She didn't sign that."
Sergeant shrugged; he had protocols, not sensor nets for forgery.

The door cracked open.
A junior constable handed the sergeant a phone slip.
"Call for Mr. Schwarz. Journalistin."

Lucas lunged, but cuffs anchored.
Sergeant set the phone on speaker.
Petra's voice bled static.
"Lucas? They pulled the article. My site—SQL wiped, backups corrupted. Our cloud keys invalidated."
"Are you okay?" Lucas asked.

"Shaken. Editor furious."
Her tone faltered, regained steel.
"I still have raw files offline. But print run spiked an error. Plates replaced."

Lucas breathed through clenched teeth.
"You're the only witness left."
"I've reached two prosecutors; both say chain of evidence broken."
She cursed under breath.
"They flagged you unstable. Appeals tough."

Sergeant muted speaker, eyes assessing.
"Friend of yours?"

"Journalist," Lucas said.

"She can confirm I'm not delusional."

Sergeant sighed—sincerity's weight heavy on him.

"Everyone says that."

He unmuted.

Petra's voice lower: "I'll keep digging, Lucas. Don't let them medicate you again."

"You keep safe," Lucas whispered before the sergeant severed the line.

Blood rushed in ears.

Lucas stared at fluorescent ballast, counting flickers: one, one, two, three, five—

Pattern carried him above panic.

Sergeant rubbed temple.

"I can hold you seventy-two hours on psychiatric hold, or you cooperate with evaluation."

Lucas inhaled.

"Cooperate."

He needed time outside a padded cell to find Petra, to salvage proof.

—

They locked him in a holding room—no bed, only bench, a steel toilet half hidden behind a partition too short for dignity.

Hours leaked; he reviewed each memory, anchoring like knots in rope.

When the door clicked and Dr. Schreiber entered—a city psych consultant—Lucas greeted him calmly.

Interview began predictable: orientation, hallucinations, threat assessment.

Lucas answered measured, referencing recent stress, acknowledging anxiety but not delusion.

He described deep-fake evidence, server wipes, SOMA security deck.

Schreiber's eyes pivoted between concern and skepticism.

"You realize high-level conspiracies require extraordinary proof."

Lucas nodded, offered the only thing unsanitized: the silver key-drive still hidden behind ID folds, discovered during property intake, but uninterpretable without a laptop.

He requested digital forensics.

Schreiber raised brows.

"I could flag that as healthy insight—or elaborate paranoid ideation."

"Check one file," Lucas pleaded.

"GPS logs, Exif, nothing spectacular."

Schreiber promised to note it, but Lucas saw decisions forming behind his measured gaze—the desire to avoid career-staining tales of shapeshifters.

Door shut.

Lucas retreated into numbers again, thirty-four steps of hope before it curved to doubt.

—

Evening lights dimmed overhead.

Lucas's eyes burned.

A guard slid a sandwich through the slot—dry roll, slice of cheese.

He ate half, saved half in pocket; uncertain hunger tomorrow.

Minutes? Hours? He lost track until the slot clanged again.

This time a phone—his old one, screen cracked.

Note taped across: *Press play.*

He frowned, peeled tape, tapped the lone video file.

Petra appeared, face lit by laptop glow.

"My systems compromised. I'm sending raw drive to three papers. But your statement is missing. They demand direct record."

She inhaled.

"You need out. Tomorrow hearing at District Court. I'll stall with injunction. Find your own words, Lucas. Truth is a shield only if spoken."

Video ended.

He stared at the cracked glass, reflection ugly, eyes haunted, but alive.

He pressed fist to heart, once, vow of solidity.

Guard hammered again.

"Phone time over."

Lucas pocketed the half-roll, surrendered phone.

Before the door closed he said, "Tell the sergeant. I'll take the stand."

Guard snorted—didn't care—but Lucas heard his boots fade down corridor.

He sat cross-legged on concrete, back straight,

breathing slow.

Sequence repeated: one, one, two, three, five, eight, thirteen, twenty-one, thirty-four, fifty-five—numbers stretching into room like scaffolding.

He climbed them, rung by rung, up through fear, into a vantage where Lea's flawless surfaces cracked under their own geometry.

Tomorrow he would speak, evidence in hand or mouth empty, mind clear.

Police flags could claim insanity.

Servers could purge.

Articles could vanish.

But a human voice, steady under oath, still had gravity. And for the first time since the ring cooled on the bedside table, he believed his words might weigh enough to bend the orbit of those who thought reality was theirs to edit.

Lights clicked off at 23:00.

Room sank to half-dark.

Lucas lay on bench, unslept but calm, half-roll under his head, silver key-drive still tucked inside stitched lining.

Heartbeat loud, sure.

He whispered the numbers once more, letting them tether him, counting through the hush.

Weighed each breath like a stone he could hurl into tomorrow's silence, sure it would make ripples no algorithm could erase.

CHAPTER 13

THE ARCHIVE

Lucas lived inside the city's cheapest hostel, room 22, top floor, mold threading the corners.
Nine bunks, four occupied by itinerant students who smelled of clove cigarettes and instant noodles.
He chose the top bunk nearest the fire escape; an exit mattered more than comfort.

He stayed invisible.
No name at desk, cash only, passport left in a side street locker.
He shaved at night, wore a knit cap, let stubble return by morning, a new face each elevator ride.
If he left, he kept a folded discharge slip in pocket—proof he was "voluntary."
If the police knocked, he would claim tourism, jet-lag, an airline misrouting.

Days blurred into bus station coffee, library terminals, burner phones swapped weekly.
Petra's newsroom moved underground, printing only in PDF newsletters now, zipped, encrypted, passed by signal groups.
Her voice came through once a day, an anchor line in a gale:

"Evidence grows, but we need one clean strike.
Stay breathing."

He tried.
He swallowed hostel toast, unremarkable broth, kept
the blue capsules hidden in a sock, flushed one each
dawn to mimic compliance if tests came.
Night descended early; he listened to bunkmate snores
and replayed yesterday's failures, tomorrow's plans.

On a Wednesday that smelled of melting snow, a new
email landed in his dead inbox—address he hadn't
used since grad school.
Subject: **"thought you'd want this // S."**
No body, only a 4-minute MP3 attachment.

He scanned it on a borrowed Chromebook, hesitant
fingers above the spacebar.
He played it.

Static first, then Julia's voice, unmistakable timbre
softened by distance.
She spoke Czech, quick phrases; Lucas's brain
translated on the run.

> "Prague is burnt.
> Next plan is the house by the river.
> Same drop, same procedure.
> We finish by solstice."

A man's voice answered, low, blurred by wind.
Coordinates rattled—five numbers North, five East.
The recorder—maybe a phone in a pocket—rustled
against fabric.
Julia again:

"No audits.

No witnesses this time."

Click.

Silence.

Lucas felt his ribs tighten like belts.

He scrubbed back, wrote the numbers on the hostel
receipt: **50.2137, 13.7504.**

Quick browser search: a rural stretch near the Ohře
River, northwest Czechia, border of black pine forest,
nearest village called Nová Lada.

He Googled *vacation homes*; a single listing from the
early two-thousands, long offline, title: **"Starý Mlýn —
Old Mill Cottage."**

One thumbnail showed cracked stucco, moss on
shingles, shutters ajar.

He leaned away.

A location off grid.

No CCTV, only trees.

A perfect vault.

Petra answered his call on third buzz.

He explained.

She whistled.

"I can't get there until Monday. Court motion."

"I'll go tonight," Lucas said.

Silence, then:

"Take body cam. Backup to cloud every hour. If you go
dark, I pull sirens."

He promised.

Heartbeat already sprinting.

He packed: DSLR, power bank, a slim crowbar from a hardware stall, flashlight, two burner phones, the silver key-drive on lanyard under his shirt, passport photocopy, thirty blue capsules still hidden.
He left the hostel at sunset, slipping twenty crowns under the pillow for luck.

Car share no questions asked: he rented a scratched gray Škoda Octavia, cash deposit, forged work letter.
Road unfurled north, city lights shedding behind him until only headlights carved tunnels through fog.
Radio played folk songs; he shut it off.
Thoughts louder: what if Julia waited with tranquilizer darts, or worse, a file-shredder running hot, ready to smoke every answer?

He crossed into Ore Mountains foothills, snowbanks rising along shoulders, moon bruised yellow behind cloud.
At 02:11 the GPS announced arrival.
Trees hemmed a narrow track down to the river—tires skidded on frost; he let momentum glide, engine low.

Old Mill appeared under the beams: two stories, boarded windows, stone wheelhouse canted sideways, moss thick as carpet.
Nobody.
No lights.
He killed the engine, waited.

Silence living, not dead—the kind that listens back.
No chain bark of guard dog, no glow of cigarette.
Just the river's hush under ice.

He zipped parka, shouldered bag, gripped crowbar.
Snow compacted under boots, loud then muffled.
Front door padlocked, chain rusted, but the latch was
replaced recently—bright metal, new screws.
Someone visited.
He slid the crowbar under the hasp, leveraged slow;
metal squealed, popped.
Heart hammered triple tempo.
Door creaked inward, sigh of long memory.

Air smelled of damp wood, mouse droppings, lemon
cleanser—fresh.
He flicked the flashlight to low beam.
Hallway narrow, walls paneled cedar.
Dust drifted, yet footprints near the door looked new:
tread of city boots, size small.
Julia's?

He stepped.
Floorboards moaned softly.
He listened.
No echo upstairs.
He advanced room to room: kitchen stripped to bones;
a single mug on the counter, lipstick ghost.
He pocketed it in evidence bag.

Back hall opened onto lounge: fireplace blackened, ash
litter.
Beside the hearth, a folding camp table, laptop closed,
external hard drive blinking amber.
Live.
He startled, raised crowbar, but room empty.
Laptop screen saver float—SOMA emblem.

No password prompt.
Odd.

He slid glove, touched trackpad.
Desktop flashed: folder tree open to
/ARCHIVE/PHASE$_4$/FINAL.
Files: **IDs**, **Contracts**, **Audio**, **Photos**, **Medical**,
Scripts.
He plugged his power bank, clicked Photos.

Thumbnails filled grid like a mosaic of stolen lives:
passports, selfies, romantic candids, clandestine
hospital corridors labeled by date.
At far right, he saw his own face—Berlin rooftop—Julia
half-visible, marking pen scrawl in red: **"ENDGAME."**
He opened it.
Her handwriting underlined his jaw: **"Done."**

Stomach pitched.
He scrolled; more of him: sleeping profile, shower
silhouette, typed email drafts—all timestamped months
before they met.
She'd surveilled, scripted lines, predicted responses.
A folder inside: **PSY_OPTS**—documents forging his
psychiatric flag, sample doctor signatures.
He felt vertigo.

He selected all, started compressing to upload.
Connection circle spun—no signal.
Of course.
He clipped body cam to parka lapel, red LED blinking,
local record.

He swapped his phone to satellite mode, still nothing.
Mountains blocked lines.

He pocketed drive.
Next folder: **IDs**.
Hundreds of high-res scans.
He opened randomly: U.K. passport **Sophia Cannon**,
U.S. driver license **Julia Cross**, Swiss ID **Lara
Novaková**, all with the same cheekbones adjusted by
hair, makeup, year.
Expirations staggered through 2030.
Production schedule.

He shot photos of screen, each key set, each page.
Crowbar set down, hands flying.
He must finish before owner returned.

A noise upstairs—footstep, faint.
He froze, flashlight killed, listened.
Another creak, above hallway.
Heartbeat cannoned.
He pocketed phone, grabbed crowbar, edged toward
staircase.

Second floor smelled of lavender soap.
Flash off, he relied on moonlight slant through broken
slat.
Bedroom door ajar.
Inside, clothesline strung end to end, clips holding
prints: large format photographs, developing curl still
visible.
He stepped in.
Pictures danced in draft:

—Havel in scrubs, date circled.—Petra leaving court, target circle.—Anton in café, scribble: **"survives— monitor."**—Lucas driving his Škoda tonight, timestamp fifteen minutes prior.

His breath stopped.
She knew he was here.
Even now lens might be on him.

On the dresser lay twin passports.
One German, one Czech, both unissued.
Photos blank—white space ready for lamination.
Beside them, an open ledger.
Row read:

> **SUBJECT:** LUIS S.
> **STATUS:** DONE
> **CLEANSE:** IN PROGRESS
> **BACKUP HOST:** T 12/06

He flipped page: next line **JOURNALIST:** P. ČERNÁ — *PEND*
A column titled **FAILSAFE** scribbled with a hospital name in Leipzig.

Lucas's spine iced.
Plan B for Petra if publishing failed.
Lea erased by removing all who might speak.

He pocketed ledger.
Noise downstairs—a door closing.
He ducked behind hanging prints, crouched.

Footfalls padded into lounge, laptop lid snapped shut.
A woman's voice low, crisp:

"Battery 50. Running mirror sync. Remove power in ten."

Radio static reply—male.

She answered in English.

"Lucas is a liability. If encountered, tranquilize. Psychiatric hold still best optic."

Lucas's mouth dried.

He gripped crowbar until knuckles ached.

He needed exit and evidence.

He scanned room: back window half boarded but rotted.

He wedged crowbar, pried quietly; wood groaned, but conversation below masked it.

He slipped ledger, flash drive into inside pocket, dropped to porch roof, snow puffing.

Cold sliced lungs.

He slid down drainpipe, boots crunching behind hedge.

Inside, voices grew sharper—argument.

He crept along house side to riverbank where Škoda waited behind spruce.

Keys in, engine cough loud; he cursed, turned ignition again—roar.

Inside lights flared; silhouettes rushed porch.

He floored reverse, gravel spraying.

One figure aimed light; a pop—gun?

Rear window spider-cracked.

He ducked, accelerated toward road.

Tires fishtailed, caught, sped into forest track.

Branches slapped windshield.

He drove blind curves, heart bass drum.

After five kilometers he killed headlights, crawled until far enough.
Pulled into the copse, engine off.

Hands trembled, but ledger pressed firm under coat, drive warm near heart, body cam still blinking.
He texted Petra: **"Archive found. Sorry. Hunted. Upload soon."**
No bars.
He cursed, restarted the phone, nothing.
Mountains.

He breathed, counted: one, one, two… slowing pulse.
Images seared mind: photo of him labeled "Done," ledger marking Petra next.
He had to warn her.
He needed net signal.
He started engine, crept south until hillside opened.
One bar.
He parked, typed again, attached cam footage snippet.
Send failed once, twice, then green check.
Relief stabbed tears to eyes.

Answer came ten minutes later: **"Get to Dresden. Safe house. We'll publish all."**
He nodded to the glowing screen as if she could see.

He resumed drive, thinking of the ledger: data on vanishings tight as medical charts, each life a clinical trial.
He glimpsed his own row again, printed in memory:
DONE.
But he was still breathing.

Still unsanitized.

That line was wrong.

Maybe other lines wrong too.

He would crack them open, broadcast, turn Old Mill into crime scene lit by a thousand phone flashes.

Snow thickened.

Wind rose.

He angled mirror and saw endless black road behind, no headlights, then maybe one far distant, could be a plow, could be pursuit.

Didn't matter.

He pressed the accelerator.

Ahead lay a border, a city, a journalist with unshredded will, and presses that still answered ink.

Behind lay the archive of a ghost—her fortress, finally mapped.

He whispered numbers to keep wheel steady, voice raw:

One. One. Two. Three. Five. Eight. Thirteen. Twenty-one. Thirty-four.

And forty-five more if breath held.

The Škoda's heater coughed warm; dawn bruised the sky ahead.

He drove toward it, pictures and plans rattling in the glove box like seeds inside a gourd, ready to spill onto ground where deletion failed, where living testimony grew roots too tangled for even her to rip out clean.

CHAPTER 14

THE NEEDLE

The engine cooled in the driveway.
Lucas gripped the wheel.
Fingers numb.
Heartbeat fast.
The world outside still blurred from exhaustion.
He looked up at the house again.
Dark windows stared back blankly.
The Old Mill stood quiet.
Snow lightly dusted its roof.
The river behind whispered secrets to no one.

He rubbed his eyes.
Sleep clawed at him, pulling him down.
He couldn't risk leaving without checking once more—
checking for something he'd missed. Something buried
deeper. Something definitive.
The archive still buzzed in his mind.
His own face, stamped with red ink: *Done.*
But he wasn't done yet.
Not until he found her.

He opened the door.
The cold bit through his clothes instantly.
He pulled the jacket tighter.

Breath fogged the air.
Carefully, quietly, he stepped toward the house again.

The broken door still hung ajar.
Inside, the stale air greeted him like an old enemy.
The living room remained exactly as he'd left it—
computer gone dark, the empty chair pushed back.
Nothing moved.
Nothing stirred.

But now, the hair at the back of his neck rose.
Something different.
A faint scent lingered, unmistakable.
Bergamot, lavender—her.

His heart clenched tight.
Pulse quickened.
Lucas turned slowly.

She stood in the doorway.
Silhouetted by moonlight.
A suitcase held casually by her side, as if arriving home
from a short trip.
Her coat impeccably tailored.
Hair darker now, swept neatly away from her face.
The same calm eyes that haunted every sleepless
hour.

"Julia." His voice cracked.

She stepped into the room, setting the suitcase down
carefully.
"I told you," she said softly. "It's not Julia."

He swallowed hard.
"Lea, then. Lara, Sophie, Karolina—does it matter anymore?"

She smiled faintly.
"No. I suppose not."

Lucas stood frozen, pulse hammering in his throat.
"You erased me. Took everything."

She tilted her head slightly, studying him as though reading a familiar but faded map.
"I'm sorry you feel that way." Her voice calm, gentle, as if explaining a minor misunderstanding.

He stepped closer, anger flaring hot behind his ribs.
"You're sorry? You made me a ghost."

"Lucas," she whispered, her voice almost pleading, "I never intended to harm you. You were never supposed to end up here."

"Then what was I?" His breath shook. "Just another case file?"

Her gaze softened momentarily.
"No. You were more than that."

He moved nearer, so close he could smell the faint scent of lavender soap and bergamot perfume—the same scents she'd worn those first nights in Berlin, when he'd thought love was real.
"You lied about everything," he said softly. "Every word. Every look."

"Not every look," she replied gently, eyes flickering with something unreadable, distant sadness maybe, or regret. "Not every word."

She reached out, fingertips brushing lightly against his chest.
He tensed but didn't pull away.
Her touch—warm, impossibly familiar—sent a tremor down his spine.
She stepped closer still, gaze locked with his.

"Lucas," she whispered, her voice a soft current pulling him under. "I really liked you."

Her lips brushed the side of his neck, barely grazing his skin.
A ghost's kiss.
His breath hitched sharply.

Then—a sudden, tiny pressure.
A sharp sting in the middle of his back.
Needle-thin, swift as a snakebite.
Panic surged instantly.
He jerked away, stumbling backward.

"What did you—"

Heat spread rapidly through his veins, racing outward from the prick.
His legs weakened, knees threatening to buckle.

She stepped back, eyes calm, almost clinical.
"I'm sorry, Lucas. You left me no choice."

His vision blurred.
The room spun lazily around him, gravity shifting,

sliding sideways.
He tried to move, to speak, but limbs felt alien—
disconnected, numb.

He collapsed onto the worn carpet, gasping.
Chest tight.
Pulse exploding in his ears, roaring louder with each
frantic beat.

She knelt calmly beside him, her face composed, gaze
distant yet sad.
"You were the only one," she whispered softly, leaning
closer, voice trembling almost imperceptibly, "the only
one who got too close."

The ceiling darkened.
Edges faded.
Blackness pooled inward like ink bleeding into paper.
He fought against it, limbs twitching uselessly, mouth
opening but no sound emerging.

"Please," he gasped. "Julia…"

She placed a hand gently against his cheek.
A caress of cold comfort.
"I'm not her. Not anymore."

Then darkness swallowed him whole.

Slowly, sensation returned.
Cold first—sharp, bitter.
Then silence, deep and absolute.

He lay motionless, eyelids heavy as stone.
Breathing shallow.
Pain throbbed distantly, like memory just out of reach.

He opened his eyes to near-total darkness.
Ceiling shadows hung low, the room unfamiliar, oppressive.
A cellar, perhaps, or basement.
Concrete floor cold beneath him.

His head spun violently as he tried to sit up.
Limbs sluggish.
Heart fluttered weakly.
He pressed hands to the freezing ground, struggling upright.

The air smelled damp, metallic—rust and mold and something chemical, medicinal.
Faint outlines emerged as vision cleared slightly:
shelves against walls, vague shapes draped in sheets.

He moved forward, legs trembling with each step.
Reaching out blindly, fingers brushed rough fabric.
He tugged it gently.

The sheet fell away, revealing shelves stacked meticulously with cardboard boxes.
Labels handwritten neatly: names, dates, locations—each a small archive of lives dissected.

Lucas stumbled backward.
Dizziness flared again.
He grasped another cloth, pulling desperately, each revelation another blow:

Marco Galilei.
Sebastian Krutý.
Jakub Havel.
Nadim Heiss.
Anton Weiss.
And then—
Lucas Schwarz.

His own box sat waiting.
He reached, hands shaking violently, opened the lid.
Inside: photos of himself from every angle, stolen moments cataloged, analyzed.
Printed emails, voice recordings, forged medical notes—every detail woven into a false history.

His heart hammered harder.
Beneath these papers, a photo album, leather-bound, embossed initials: J.S.
He opened it slowly.
Images flashed vividly—Julia smiling, posing, always beside someone new.
Different men.
Different cities.
Identities shifted seamlessly, hair colors, clothes, lives.

At the very end: one photo, solitary, placed carefully.
Himself on their apartment balcony, smiling toward the camera.
In her familiar handwriting beneath, two words:

"Last one."

Breath caught painfully.
He closed the album.

She'd planned this from the first moment.
He was never real to her.
Only another file.

Light flickered behind him suddenly, the cellar door above creaking open.
Footsteps descended slowly, calm, deliberate.

He turned weakly, leaning against the shelving.
Julia—no, Lea—appeared in the dim glow, descending gracefully.
Her face calm, unreadable, eyes reflecting pale lamplight.

She stopped, studying him quietly.
"You're awake sooner than expected."

He swallowed, throat dry. "Why are you doing this?"

She tilted her head. "Everyone has secrets, Lucas. Secrets they bury, secrets they'd kill to hide."

"And you? What secrets?"

She smiled faintly. "Secrets that buy influence. Secrets that rewrite identities, create new lives, erase old ones."

"You destroy lives."

"No," she said gently. "I curate them. You never noticed the seams until I let you."

He shook his head, anger rising again. "And you?"

She sighed softly, almost regretfully. "I have no seams anymore. I erased mine first."

He stared at her, pulse drumming. "Was anything ever real?"

She hesitated—a rare break in her composure. "Some moments. Briefly."

He took a shaky step forward. "Tell me your real name."

She looked away. "It doesn't matter."

"It does," he whispered fiercely.

She met his eyes again, expression unreadable. "Karolina was close enough."

He breathed in sharply. "The girl who vanished years ago."

"The first version," she admitted. "The first erasure."

His limbs trembled, energy draining fast. The drug still burning through his veins, toxic heaviness returning.

"You can't keep erasing," he said weakly.

"Why not?" she asked softly. "It's a skill. Some people paint. Some write. I erase."

"Lives aren't paint," he rasped.

She smiled sadly, stepping close again, fingertips brushing his cheek. "All lives are paint, Lucas. Temporary, beautiful, fleeting."

He flinched, but couldn't pull away fully. Her touch hypnotic even now, warmth masking poison beneath.

"You could stop," he said desperately. "We could leave. Together. Start again."

Her eyes flickered with something—sorrow perhaps, or genuine regret. "You know I can't."

"Then kill me," he whispered bitterly. "Finish it cleanly."

She shook her head gently. "That's not how erasure works. Death leaves marks. Questions. Evidence."

"So what happens now?"

"Now," she said, voice soft again, controlled, gentle, "you go quietly. Forgotten, piece by piece, memory by memory, until you're just a whispered ghost in empty rooms."

He closed his eyes, heart aching dully. "Please."

She leaned in, lips brushing his ear. "You'll never find me again. That's mercy, Lucas."

Her footsteps retreated softly.
Stairs creaked as she ascended, door shutting gently above.

Lucas sank slowly to the concrete again, limbs leaden. Cold seeping in.
Pulse slowing.
Darkness pooling once more.

Above him, the faint hum of machinery—servers purging data, drives overwriting memories, digital lives dissolving.
He tried to summon strength, to stand again, to fight.

But energy faded.
Vision dimmed.
Thoughts fractured slowly, slipping away.

As consciousness ebbed, one image remained vivid—
Julia's face on their balcony, smiling gently, eyes soft, a memory he knew she'd erase next.
The last shred of a life she'd built just to dismantle.

Darkness whispered forward, swallowing him again.
He let go finally, exhausted, slipping quietly toward oblivion, her final words repeating softly, gently, lovingly.

CHAPTER 15

CONSENT

Snow veiled the Old Mill for seven silent days.
No new tire tracks scored the frozen lane.
No smoke drifted from its crumbling chimney.
The river kept its secrets beneath a thin, silver crust.
A pair of hikers found the body by mistake—an off-trail
detour, a curiosity about an abandoned wheelhouse.

They broke a pane, crawled inside, and smelled the
stillness first—stale air, faint lemon cleanser, dust.
Then they saw him.
Lucas lay on the guest-room cot, hands folded loosely
on his chest, as if placed there by a careful attendant.
Eyes half-open, fixed on the cracked plaster ceiling.
No blood.
No bruises.
No marks but a pinprick scar on the left side of his
back, half-hidden by the shirt collar.
Room otherwise bare: one chair, a wool blanket folded
at the foot, an overturned mug on the floor, its rim
smudged with dried lipstick.

Police arrived before dusk.
Flash cameras stuttered against the peeling wallpaper.
They bagged everything: the mug, the blanket, the
crowbar against the skirting board, a handful of

scattered Polaroids still curling on a sill.
They taped off the door.
A detective muttered the usual questions: forced entry? struggle? robbery?
None fit.
The front lock was broken, yes, but that could have been days old.
The rest of the house, though dusty, showed a strange order—boxes labeled neatly, laptop cables coiled, papers stacked by the fireplace.
Someone had kept tidy while death slipped in.

The coroner's preliminary note read like a shrug:—
Body temperature consistent with death four to six days prior.—No external violence.—No signs of prolonged suffocation.
Blood work revealed only a faint chemical fingerprint— unknown compound, molecular structure fragmentary, half-metabolized into something untraceable.
Toxicologists ran a battery of mass-spectrometry sweeps.
They found a narrow spike, but it matched no scheduled poison, no recreational narcotic, no pharmaceutical patent.
The official report froze at *undetermined causality*.
Suicide, under influence of "novel psychoactive substance," lodged itself into the margins because the alternative—murder by phantom compound—made the case too heavy for winter budgets.

In the press write-up, Lucas became a footnote:
Berlin novelist found dead in Czech countryside.

A troubled creative.

A history of mental-health concerns.

The journalist who tried to print his story, Petra Černá, mailed the editor a withering letter:

"This man was not a cliché."

But the editor trimmed her protest to a single bland pull-quote: *"Friends say he had felt unstable."*

The newsroom moved on to brighter tragedies.

On the fourth day after the discovery, **Dr. Lara Novaková** sat in an interview room at the district station in Karlovy Vary.

Fluorescent tubes hummed overhead, washing the walls the color of curdled milk.

She wore a gray turtleneck, no jewelry, hair tucked behind her ears with surgical neatness.

A plain winter coat hung on the chair beside her.

Her suitcase—small, practical—rested by her feet.

She wrapped chilled fingers around a paper cup of tea.

Detective Jiří Sedláček read from a thin file.

"According to the innkeeper in Prague, you were the last to see Mr. Schwarz alive."

Her hands trembled once—tiny, controlled.

"Yes," she said.

"He called me three times that week. I was worried."

She glanced down, eyelashes shuttering for half a breath.

"He'd been… incoherent. Conspiracies. I thought it best to meet him."

"You met at a café."

She nodded.

"He was agitated. Paranoid. He accused me of stealing his identity. Of plotting to erase him. It was impossible to reason with him."

Her voice cracked, perfectly.

"I tried to calm him. I truly did."

Detective Sedláček studied her—voice recorder ticking, pen still.

"You left the café, called police."

A slow nod.

"I feared he might hurt himself. Or others."

She wiped a tear that glimmered on cue.

"Was that wrong?"

He asked about the Old Mill.

She feigned surprise—an earnest widening of eyes.

"I hadn't been there in years. My grandfather owned it once. I let Lucas stay when he said he needed solitude. I thought it safe."

No tremor in the lie.

The detective slid photos across—Lucas on the cot, half-shadowed.

She covered her mouth, eyes glassing over.

A practiced grief, but Sedláček had seen worse performances that still rang true.

"For toxicology, we need context," he said gently.

"Did Mr. Schwarz use drugs?"

"He talked about sleeping pills," she whispered.

"Hallucinations."

Another pause.

"I worried he might self-medicate."
He wrote that down.
Unstable subject. Potential narcotics. Suicide plausible.

She signed the statement in precise loops.
They thanked her for cooperation, said they might call
again.
She stood, slipped her coat on, lifted the suitcase
handle with steady fingers.

Outside the station, afternoon light glazed wet
cobblestones.
Snowmelt trickled in gutters.
She crossed the small square toward the train terminal,
her steps unhurried.

**

The ticket hall smelled of diesel and cinnamon pastry.
Departure board flickered: **EC 174 to Vienna – 16:08 –
platform 3.**
She purchased a second-class fare in cash, no loyalty
card.
Walked down the long ramp, suitcase wheels clicking in
measured rhythm.
The train idled, idling breath of iron and oil.
She found an almost empty compartment near the rear.

A middle-aged man sat by the window, typing on a
tablet.
Gray tweed coat, balding crown, gentle academic
slouch.
He looked up, polite half-smile.
She gestured to the opposite seat.

"Is this seat still free?"

English, soft accentless.

He straightened, returning a courteous nod.

"Please."

She stowed the suitcase overhead, removed her coat, folded it precisely, placed it on the rack.

The train lurched into motion.

Fields rolled by—sleek, winter-worn.

Inside the compartment the man resumed typing, unaware of the quiet strategist across from him.

She opened a small paperback—foreign poetry, blank inside covers.

Between its pages lay a single micro-SD card.

She slid it discreetly into the lining of her wallet.

Minutes passed.

She closed the book, set it aside, and studied her reflection in the window—floating over blurred farmland.

Brown hair, calm eyes, just another traveler.

Lucas's face flickered in the glass, as memories sometimes did, but she blinked it away.

The man glanced up.

She offered a gentle smile.

"Tight deadlines?"

He chuckled, easing the tension of strangers.

"Always. Conference paper."

"What field?"

"Behavioral economics."

Curiosity brightened her gaze.

"Fascinating," she murmured.

"Do you mind explaining a bit?"
He set the tablet down, eager to share.

She listened, nodding with genuine interest.
Questions well-timed, encouraging.
He warmed quickly, words flowing.
Trust blossomed in less than twenty minutes.
She learned his name, his university, his favorite place
for espresso in Vienna.
She laughed softly at his jokes—music of comfort.

At one point he asked hers.
She smiled, eyes steady.
"Anna."
No surname offered.
He didn't press.
People rarely did.

Outside, dusk deepened.
Inside, conversation rolled on smooth rails.
The man spoke of models and incentives, unaware he
was mapping his own vulnerabilities at every anecdote,
revealing soft points, desires, fears.
She recorded nothing, needed no devices; memory
trained to catalog effortlessly.

The train rocked gently.
Lights flickered on overhead.
"Anna" excused herself, returning moments later with
two cups of tea.
She placed one before him.
A simple gesture of kindness.

He thanked her, surprised.

Steam curled between them, warmth shared.

They sipped, silence settling companionably.

The man returned to his tablet.

She opened the book again, scanning blank pages.

After a time, she looked out at night-dark fields.

Thoughts drifted backward for a heartbeat—Berlin mornings, Lucas humming off-key while brewing strong coffee, sunlight across their shared kitchen.

A tenderness flickered, brief, then folded away like a letter burned at the edges.

She reminded herself: attachments weaken the algorithm.

She'd let one grow too long.

The cost was unavoidable.

Lesson reinforced.

The train glided toward Vienna, lights of remote farms blinking like low stars.

"Anna" finished her tea, set the cup firmly on the tray.

Tomorrow she would be someone else.

Perhaps in Zurich, perhaps in Madrid.

She hadn't chosen yet.

But tonight, under the soft hum of European rails, she simply sat, a quiet woman in a clean coat, traveling toward a new chapter, a new canvas.

Outside, the darkness streamed past.

Inside, the compartments clicked and swayed, a perfect machine.

And somewhere, in a morgue drawer near Karlovy Vary, Lucas lay still—officially a tragic self-inflicted demise, chemically enigmatic, no one to contest the narrative except a journalist whose servers kept crashing and a handful of scattered files the authorities called inadmissible.

The train horn sounded, long and low.
The journey continued.
She closed her eyes, leaning back, smelling faint bergamot on her scarf.
The man beside her had returned to typing.
He would finish his paper, present at a conference, shake hands.
Perhaps he'd receive an email someday from a curious woman named Anna who shared a passion for incentives.
A friendship might spark.
Opportunities might arise.

She considered it calmly, coolly, the way a chess player weighs future moves.
The board always resets.
The pieces change, the patterns persist.

Outside the window a field of dark snow blurred by, a blank page awaiting the first stroke of new ink.

And the train rolled on.

Printed in Dunstable, United Kingdom